SHE WANTED THE DUKE AS A FATHER—NOT AS A HUSBAND

Lady Juliet Manchester felt it her duty to make the Duke of Severn a father—to the twin daughters he already had. For since the death of his wife, Severn had most shamefully neglected his offspring Anne and Amelia as he pursued his endless round of pleasures in London and abroad, leaving the girls to grow up in the country unwanted and wild.

But how could she induce the domineering duke to do this duty as a parent without a wife to give him the aid and advice he so clearly needed? It was a question Juliet found devilishly difficult to answer. Since the price for saving those two darling girls from utter ruin was one she dreaded to have to pay . . .

The Dreadful Duke

More Regency Romances from SIGNET

The Dreadful Duke

by

Barbara Hazard

A SIGNET BOOK

NEW AMERICAN LIBRARY

NAL BOOKS ARE AVAILABLE AT QUANTITY DISCOUNTS WHEN USED
TO PROMOTE PRODUCTS OR SERVICES. FOR INFORMATION PLEASE
WRITE TO PREMIUM MARKETING DIVISION, NEW AMERICAN
LIBRARY, 1633 BROADWAY, NEW YORK, NEW YORK 10019.

 SIGNET TRADEMARK REG—U.S.PAT.OFF. AND FOREIGN COUNTRIES
REGISTERED TRADEMARK—MARCA REGISTRADA
HECHO EN CHICAGO, U.S.A.

SIGNET, SIGNET CLASSIC, MENTOR, PLUME, MERIDIAN and NAL BOOKS
are published by New American Library,
1633 Broadway, New York, New York 10019

First Printing, November, 1985

1 2 3 4 5 6 7 8 9

PRINTED IN THE UNITED STATES OF AMERICA

1

The Duke of Severn shifted his weight so he might bend his knee to ease his tired muscles. He felt as if he had been standing immobile for hours, all his not inconsiderable weight on his left leg, but he knew that if he called this to the attention of the rapt artist who was painting his portrait, he would receive little sympathy. As he moved, an impatient order came from behind the large canvas. "Kindly hold the pose, your Grace. I have reached a difficult section."

"I pray you will conquer it before I succumb to the infirmities of old age," he said in his usual sarcastic drawl.

An absentminded "hmmm" was his only reply.

The duke bit back a sharp retort and tried to find something interesting in the paneling on the wall of the studio where he had been ordered to direct his gaze. He remembered that it was he who had suggested the pose; he could hardly quarrel with his own choice now.

He could hear himself saying, "Yes, by all means let us do the thing up right for posterity. It must be a full-length portrait, of course. I shall wear formal dress and stand with my hand resting on some papers—important affairs of state, naturally—that will be on a table at my side. Let me think . . . Ah, yes, my other hand shall be on my hip. Of course, the right leg must be extended and my gaze fixed on something in the distance as if I were pondering the fate of the nation." He had laughed at his fancies then. "Typical, is it not? I find I am as vain as any man, and so I insist on being portrayed larger than life and in a heroic mode. What a shame I cannot wear full regimentals with my chest covered by medals while I grasp the hilt of a sword. If only I had realized this moment was inevitable, I would have enlisted at some point in my misspent youth."

As his host and hostess had joined in his mocking laughter, he had added, "But at least no one will ever know the important papers that apparently I have been perusing are nothing but old bills of sale and one of Andrew's stud books."

Now, to distract himself from his aching muscles, the duke let his mind range over the events that had brought him here. He had been traveling abroad for almost a year, and a few weeks after his return to England, he had been invited to visit Blagdon. Since he had not seen the marquess and marchioness for such a long time, he had accepted with pleasure. He might dislike country living, but in the years since their marriage, Claire and Andrew Tyson had become his very good friends.

A fly buzzed somewhere near the large, north-lit windows, and the droning sound seemed loud in the quiet room. Had it really been five years ago that the Tysons had married? It did not seem that long, but there were two babies in the nursery to confirm it, and the girl he had fancied himself in love with at one time had a new air of maturity about her. He thought her more beautiful than ever, her face serene and content, although he found he missed the short black curls she had once sported. Now her hair was drawn back into a large chignon, befitting her matronly status. For a moment he felt a stab of regret for what might have been, and he sighed. She had loved Andrew Tyson then as she did now, not William Fairhaven, and there had not been a thing he could do to change her mind.

6

The duke sighed again, more audibly this time. His left knee was beginning to tremble with the strain of holding the pose.

"Only a few minutes more, your Grace," the artist murmured, intent on the canvas.

"I know your 'few minutes,' Claire," he retorted. "If I were not positive that this portrait will surpass any in England, I would withdraw the commission immediately. You are a slave driver, ma'am."

Lady Blagdon's face appeared from behind the canvas, and she grinned at him, wrinkling her nose as she did so. The duke was tempted to laugh. Claire always wore an old-fashioned mob cap when she painted, and she looked the complete urchin.

The laughing face disappeared, and the duke concentrated on the pose.

"You may lower your chin, William," Claire said now, her voice abstracted again. "I am working on the left leg now."

"How unfortunate. It is the left leg that pains me," the duke remarked, as if to himself. He knew Claire did not hear a word. He had never seen anyone who became so absorbed in their work as his talented hostess. His mind returned to that London Season five years ago, and he smiled. Miss Claire Carrington had been the most singular, unusual debutante that had been seen for many a year. It was not only that she would not curtsy to her betters and seemed to have no interest in the *haut ton* or in marriage, but also because she was a talented artist who studied side by side with men in a professional's studio. He remembered the furor that had occurred when she had shown a classical painting at the Royal Academy Exhibition, a painting whose major figure, clad only in draperies, was the image of Andrew Tyson. Claire was so in love with him that, inadvertently, she had painted his face from memory. It had taken all the duke's considerable address to quiet the scandal and bring the two lovers together.

But now he had to admit he was glad he had done so, for he had seldom seen a couple so happy, so much in love. When he had arrived, he had warned them as he always did that any lovesick glances would send him on his way at once, and they had scoffed at the very idea of such behavior. But even after five years of marriage, there was that between them that caused a kind of electric current when their eyes met. When Andrew touched his wife, helping her to a chair or a seat in the carriage, the duke felt he might just as well have been invisible, for all the two of them were aware of him. He had not hesitated to call them to order sharply, but he could not help feeling regret that this kind of love, so consuming and deep and rich, had never been his good fortune to know.

He had the sudden thought that perhaps there were some men—himself among them—who were incapable of inspiring it. Perhaps there was something missing in his makeup, some serious character flaw that would not permit him to love this way, or have his love returned. A shallowness, a weakness he had never been aware of until now.

His dark eyes grew bleak as he considered this distressing possibility. He had never thought of himself as weak or shallow, and certainly there could be no question that there were few women he had wanted who had not succumbed to his considerable charm.

He had married while still young, choosing a pretty, pleasant, agreeable girl to be his duchess. Now he wondered if Anne had ever regretted the only role he had allowed her to play, as the mother of his children. Had she been satisfied with nothing but politeness and a little affection from him? Perhaps she had dreamed of the kind of love Andrew Tyson gave his wife; perhaps she had wished she might be free to return it, even as Claire did.

He had to admit, since he was being honest with himself, that her death had caused him nothing but a slight regret; certainly he had not mourned her as she deserved. And is this not the mark of a shallow man? he asked himself now. She had given so much and she had received so little from him in return.

He forced his mind from these depressing thoughts, telling himself his introspection was ridiculous. He did not think even now that there had been any hidden depths to Anne's character, and certainly she had always seemed happy. But although there had been countless opportunities, he had not repeated that matrimonial experience when he was free to do so. Instead, he had enjoyed an occasional discreet liaison with women of his own class. He had never been tempted to set up a mistress, as other men did, for that sort of arrangement had seemed rather commonplace. Besides, it was definitely beneath him. He was the Duke of Severn and, as such, did not have to pay for any woman's favors. He never had.

But the fact that he had never felt any deep commitment to another human being continued to disturb him. Could it be that he was, in reality, not the admirable, impeccable, perfect person he had always thought himself? Was it possible that, instead, he was flawed, seriously flawed?

He shook his head. He had not had such puerile doubts about himself since his adolescence. Of course he was content with his lot, his life full and rich; it was only seeing the Tysons together that had prompted such maudlin mental meanderings.

He had been at Blagdon, the Tyson seat east of Bath, for almost three weeks now. He had asked Claire to paint his portrait, claiming he must have one of her works for his gallery at Severn. True, he had purchased the one that had brought her so much notoriety, but he had given it back to them as a wedding gift.

9

Now Claire Tyson stepped back and stared at the canvas and then at him in turn. Her head was tilted to one side as she considered her work, and she scratched her mob cap unconsciously, leaving a new smear of oil paint to join the others that adorned it. At last she nodded and said, "That will be enough for today, William. I can continue without your posing any longer, although I shall need you at the same time tomorrow."

As she spoke, the door of the studio opened behind her, and the marquess came in. "No, that is enough for you today as well, my dear," he said, taking the brush and palette from her hands and pushing her gently down to rest on a tall stool. His smile was intimate as he did so.

As the duke stepped down from the model stand and stretched his tired muscles, Claire protested. "But there is only a little more to do today, Drew! You must let me finish."

The marquess bent and took her face between his hands to study it carefully. "You are sure you are all right, Claire?" he asked, his voice a caress.

She nodded as the duke strolled up to them.

"Now, what is all this about, my dears?" he asked, taking out his pocket watch to study it. "I see we have only been at work for little more than an hour. Claire is not so fragile that she must rest after such a short time, is she?"

When he saw her laughing eyes, he added, "Not that I am not delighted to be dismissed for the day, mind you. She is a hard taskmaster, Andrew."

The marquess nodded. "She is indeed, but since we expect another little Tyson to join Marion and baby Jessica in the nursery this winter, she must have a care for herself."

The duke's slashing black brows rose in surprise, and the Tysons smiled at him, not a bit self-conscious. "Another baby?" he asked. "Why, my congratulations! No wonder you insist on her stopping, my friend."

"Oh, Drew would like to wrap me up in cotton," Claire said, rising to return to the canvas. "After two children I have discovered there is nothing unusual about having a baby. It is a completely natural act."

Her eyes met her husband's for a warm, fleeting moment, and then she said, "Would you care to see how your portrait is coming along, your Grace? I am pleased with it myself."

The two men moved forward. They were always careful not to ask to inspect Claire's work until they had been invited to do so, for they knew how she hated to be watched while she worked. Now, as he studied the large canvas, the duke nodded in satisfaction.

"It is excellent, as fine as I knew it would be," he said, his admiring voice for once completely devoid of sarcasm and boredom.

Lord Blagdon studied the painting, and then the man beside him. How well Claire has caught him, he marveled. William Fairhaven, the Duke of Severn, was a tall man in his early forties and at the height of his power. He had broad shoulders, a good build, and long muscular legs, and the presence to carry off the somewhat heroic pose that, attempted by another man, would merely look contrived and theatrical. Above the white of his shirt points and cravat, his handsome aristocratic face with its piercing dark eyes stared proudly past the viewer, those slashing black brows that made his face and expression so unique, clearly defined. He was not smiling in the portrait, but Claire had caught a light in his eyes and a small twist to his sculptured mouth that seemed to reveal to any viewer that, inside, he was smiling to himself. Or was it *at* himself? the marquess mused. Anyone looking at this work, no matter how many years in the future that might be, would know that this had been a fascinating, intelligent man. The marquess suspected that members of the feminine sex would sigh as one with regret that they had not lived in the same century as this commanding, compelling duke.

He turned to compliment his wife and discovered that she had picked up her palette and was completely absorbed again, darting glances at the painting even as she mixed some fresh paint. Without a word, he took the duke's arm and led him away, closing the studio door softly behind them.

"She does not even know we have left, does she?" the duke asked, his voice amused. "How can you be sure she will not continue to paint until the light fades?"

Andrew Tyson grinned at his friend. "Never fear! I shall return in another hour and insist on it. A husband has some authority, as you know, although Claire has been very good. She says she can tell that this baby she carries is heir to Blagdon, and in spite of all her nonchalance about her pregnancy, she takes the greatest care of herself."

"I have always thought you fortunate in your choice of wife, Andrew. Indeed, I envy you," the duke remarked as the two strolled down the stairs to the library.

The marquess accepted the compliment with a nod, his good-looking face with its dark-blue eyes alight with happiness. "Yes, Claire gives me the happy ending I never thought to have, and all due to you, your Grace. I can never thank you enough for making our marriage possible."

The duke waved a careless hand. "Do not refine on it too much, my friend. I am sure you would have won her eventually. All I did was speed up the process."

He wandered over to the windows of the library as his host went to pour them both a glass of wine. It was a warm August day, and the deep shade under the elms that edged the sweeping lawns looked inviting. Although he himself had no use for the country, he had to admit the scene before him was pleasant to the eye. The gardens were in riotous, scented bloom, and the lawns seemed like a lush velvet carpet.

As he took the glass his host presented, a knock sounded on the door and the Tyson butler entered with the afternoon post on a silver salver. There was a considerable amount of it, for besides Lord Blagdon's correspondence, the duke's was being forwarded to him here for the duration of his stay.

As was their custom, the two settled down in facing armchairs to inspect their letters in a friendly silence. At length, Lord Blagdon heard the duke utter a soft oath, and he looked up to see a frown on that dark, generally enigmatic face.

"Something wrong?" Blagdon asked as the duke crumpled the letter in disgust.

"It is my daughters again," his guest explained, his frown deepening. "It always seems to be my daughters these days. I pray you will escape such hoydens with your own two girls, Drew. But then, you will have several years of serenity before you are faced with that possibility." He sighed. "I do not know what has come over them, now they have reached the age of thirteen. They were never any trouble when they were younger." He paused to sip his wine. "To be truthful, I must say I do not *think* they were. I am not at Severn very much, as you know."

The marquess wisely did not comment, although both he and his wife had often deplored the duke's casual attitude toward his five children. When his wife had died at the birth of the twin girls, after earlier presenting him with three sons, he had left his hopeful family to the care of nannies and governesses and tutors, until such time as they could be sent to school.

Will, his eldest son, was now seventeen and, with his sixteen-year-old brother Gregory, touring Greece under the tutelage of a learned cleric. At fourteen, Charles was still at Eton, but the twin girls—Anne, who had been named for her mother, and Amelia—remained at Severn. The duke supposed he must see about a school for young ladies for them in a few years, but now he wondered what school would take them, such madcaps as they appeared. As his agent had pointed out in his letter, this was the third governess who had left the estate this year in a flood of either tears or righteous indignation.

Now the duke said, his face grim, "I shall have to return to Severn as soon as the portrait is completed, Andrew, much as it pains me to do so. I may never have taken a direct hand in their upbringing before, but it appears that a stern, fatherly lecture is long overdue. I must also speak to my housekeeper, Mrs. Pomfret, to discover why she has allowed them to grow so wild. The overall care of all the children has always been her special charge, and this behavior of the girls is unlike anything she has permitted before. Perhaps she is growing too old for the task. She never had any trouble with the boys; why should two young chits be able to kick up such a rumpus?"

At the marquess's sympathetic look, he added in a drawling voice, "But why am I, of all men, surprised? Women, as I am sure you must agree, my dear friend, take great delight in being difficult at any age, be it thirteen, thirty, or a hundred and three!"

The duke was not averse to relating the twins' latest mischief to his friend, and although Andrew chuckled at the flight of the latest governess and bemoaned the loss by fire of one of the duke's tenant farmer's sheds on Midsummer's Eve, he could not help feeling a little tremor of alarm. Was this what awaited the Tysons when those two darling bits of pink chubby humanity reached their teens? He shuddered at the possibility and resolved to keep a close eye on them as soon as they were out of leading reins.

When Claire was informed of the duke's problems at dinner that evening, she shook her head, but to her husband's relief, she did not speak immediately. The duke, however, had no trouble interpreting the speculative glance she gave him.

He raised one hand and said in his sarcastic drawl, "There is no need to tell me, dear Claire. Yes, I am sure you are right, and what they really need is a mother, but I have no intention of marrying merely to provide them with a good example. In a very few years they will be married and contemplating motherhood themselves, leaving me to spend the rest of my life with the, er, good example. I am not so noble."

He paused, and his hostess said slowly, "Yes, I was thinking of a mother for your twins. But I can see it is impossible, for I am sure you will never marry again. You are much too old to change your ways now."

"Claire!" her husband scolded, looking shocked. "Mind your tongue!"

"Do you consider me too old to attract a wife, ma'am?" the duke asked stiffly, those distinctive black brows drawn together in a ferocious frown.

Claire laughed. "Are you fishing for compliments, Willam? Of course I did not mean that. You know very well how devastating and desirable you are. I daresay there isn't a single woman of your acquaintance who would not consider marriage with you a dream come true. No, I only meant that you yourself have no inclination toward that happy state."

Somewhat mollified, the duke nodded his thanks, and then he said, "I shall go to Severn and spend as much time there as is necessary to assess the problem and correct it, and then I shall engage a stricter governess. Perhaps I shall even engage two."

"Two, William?" Claire asked, a little bewildered.

"Why not?" the duke asked. "After all, there are two of *them,* and as a pair, they outnumber the most redoubtable mentor. Perhaps the good ladies would find it easier to work in shifts, as they do in the manufactories. Then, when one is at the end of her strength and patience, the other, quite refreshed and rested, can take over."

"You speak as if your daughters were wild animals to be tamed, sir," Claire admonished him. "Remember they are only little girls!"

The duke bent his dark head toward his hostess, and one black brow soared. "That is what frightens me, dear ma'am," he murmured. "If they can cause such problems now, imagine what they will be like with a few more years' experience. Why, when they make their come-out, not a bachelor in the realm will be safe."

He sipped his wine until the laughter that greeted this sally subsided, and then he said, "Unaccustomed as I am, I am sure I shall be able to find some way to control them and command their filial obedience."

Claire Tyson smiled at him. "I have no doubt of the outcome at all, your Grace. After all, as you were so quick to agree with me just now, you have always had considerable address and phenomenal success with ladies of any age, have you not?"

"Baggage!" both the duke and her husband exclaimed together, and she dissolved in laughter once again.

2

The Duke of Severn arrived at his principal seat late on a sunny, unusually sultry August afternoon a week later. He was hot and tired, for he had instructed his coachman to spring the team, having little desire to spend another night at a wayside inn. The roads this late in summer had been thick with dust, for there had not been a shower for some time, and even as elegant a vehicle as the duke's coach could not withstand the grit that crept through every available crevice. As the coach traversed the village street and paused at the tall stone pillars that marked the entrance to Severn, the duke snapped his fingers at his valet.

"A handkerchief, Marles," he ordered. His man was quick to produce a snowy linen square so his master might wipe his face while the gatekeeper opened the heavy wrought-iron gates.

As the coach traveled through them and then settled down to a smoother pace now the well-raked drive had been reached, the duke managed a smile. "I have never known it to be so hot at this time of year. I had hoped that in Devon, so near the sea, I might enjoy some respite, but it appears that that is not to be the case."

He looked idly out the window as the coach swept around a wide curve and then rumbled over the bridge that spanned one end of the large lake that fronted the hall, and suddenly his eyes grew keen. Marles was startled when he heard the duke's strangled oath and saw the way he banged the roof, ordering his coachman to halt.

The valet was still trying to right himself from the abrupt stop when the duke wrenched open the door before either of his liveried grooms could assist him. In a minute he was striding away toward the lake.

"Go on to the hall at once," he ordered over his shoulder, and obediently the coach resumed its interrupted passage. Marles peered from the window, and his eyes widened. His master was still some distance from a trio cavorting in the shallow water. As one of the smaller figures stood up, he could see she didn't have anything on but a thoroughly wet, now thoroughly transparent shift.

"My lawd," he whistled softly, sinking back on the squabs in amazement. "Nekkid females at Severn? That won't please his Grace, I *don't* think!"

The trio in the lake suddenly noticed that they were not alone, and with an identical shriek the two smaller figures waded quickly to the bank, where they had left a small pile of clothes. Once they had left the water, it could be seen they were only young girls. They were somewhat tall for their undeveloped figures, with long straight black hair now hanging damply over their thin, narrow shoulders. It was not a very good cover, and the duke knew exactly who they were.

By the time he reached this quiet corner of the lake, they had disappeared behind some hedges that marked the boundary of the formal gardens. In the distance he could hear their high-pitched giggles, and it did nothing to calm his blazing temper.

Standing on the very edge of the lake, he found himself confronting the only bather who had had the courage to remain, and the pleasant smile she gave him caused his temper to flare higher.

"Good afternoon," she called, for she had moved into deeper water at his approach and now only her head and shoulders were visible. "I assume I have the honor of addressing the Duke of Severn?"

The duke found himself sweeping his beaver from his smooth black hair and bowing before he caught himself.

18

In the lake, the lady inclined her head, and then she gave an amused chuckle. "How absurd this is," she said. "Can you imagine, I was trying to curtsy, your Grace?"

The duke's expression did not brighten as he studied her. He could not tell her age, but the poise with which she accepted this embarrassing situation revealed she was no young girl. Her thick ash-blond hair was pinned up on top of her head, showing off a well-rounded neck and soft white shoulders. He could not determine the color of her eyes, but her features were finely formed, from a determined chin, straight nose, and rosy mouth to well-arched brows. As she moved her arms, treading water, he could see the shoulder straps of a lacy chemise. She had been swimming with his daughters almost as naked as they were.

This revelation seemed to infuriate him even more, but unlike other men, when the Duke of Severn became angry, he did not raise his voice. Instead, he spoke in a cold, silken drawl, his words chosen to freeze and humiliate, rather than to burn. Now he said, "Under the circumstances, I shall not be so gauche as to inquire your name, madam. It is a matter of supreme indifference to me in any case. Yes, as you so correctly surmise, I am duke here. And you are about to join the ranks of the others who have come and gone at Severn this year. Since my agent did not mention engaging you, you cannot have been in residence long, so we must hope you have not done irremediable damage to my daughters' characters."

The lady looked confused. "I do not understand your words, sir, but from what I have seen of them, I should think that impossible. Damaging their characters, I mean."

The duke flushed. How dare such as she bandy words with him and criticize his daughters as well?

"Come out of the lake at once," he ordered, hands on hips.

"I cannot," she replied easily. The duke was not used to having any order of his disobeyed, and he stiffened. "For a very good reason I am held captive here," the lady continued. "Not that I mind, I assure you, sir. The water is delightful, so cool and refreshing. You should try it yourself sometime."

She flipped a spray of diamond drops in a curving arc, and then she looked down at herself and shook her head. "No, I must remain in the water until you have gone away."

"A pity you did not think of that before you disrobed and began your swim, madam," the duke said, his cold words measured.

"But as you can see, there was no danger of us being espied on until you arrived to disturb our idyll. We are quite out of sight of the hall and the village and gate-house as well."

The duke glanced around and saw the truth of what she said. This end of the lake curved away from the front of the hall, and there was a small wood between it and the water. The bend in the mile-long drive and a small island in the middle of the lake hid even the gate-house from view. They were quite isolated.

"Besides, no one had any inkling that you were about to make one of your infrequent visits to the ancestral acres today, sir," she continued. "You may be sure we would never have dreamed of bathing if we had had even the tiniest clue as to your whereabouts."

She smiled again, revealing even white teeth, and for the first time he noticed the brown mole set beside her mouth.

The duke was furious. The hot August sun was beating down on his shoulders and uncovered head, and he knew he was dusty and disheveled. He could feel a thin trickle of perspiration running down his back, and the uncomfortable way his cambric shirt and tight breeches were sticking to him, and the sight of her, so

cool and comfortable as she disported herself in his lake
—yes, *his* lake—was more than he could bear.

"I shall go away at once, madam," he said coldly
through gritted teeth. "And the minute I have disappeared, I expect you to leave the water, dress, and go
to your room, where you will remain secluded. Immediate arrangements shall be made to have your trunks
packed and a place reserved for you on the next stage.
Such an immodest, wanton jade is not at all the type of
female I care to have as governess for my daughters.
You are dismissed."

The lady's eyes had widened during this impassioned
speech, and her mouth had fallen open a little in
amazement. "Oh, I do beg your pardon, but you do not
understand, your Gr—"

The duke interrupted her, waving an impatient hand.
"No more!" he ordered. "I have no interest in con-
versing further with a—with you, and no intention of
changing my mind. I am sure you would not care to
have me write you a reference. I can assure you it would
be a scathing commentary on your suitability, morals,
and character."

As he concluded this daunting speech, he set his
beaver back on his smooth black hair. The damp inner
band seemed to clamp around his hot forehead like a
vise.

He was gratified by the heavy silence behind him as he
strode away, and he completely missed the two slim
figures who scampered away from the hedge where they
had hidden to watch the confrontation, and who now
disappeared around the back of the west wing.

The long, hot walk up to the hall did nothing to
improve the duke's mood. As he climbed the gentle rise
from the lake, pushed through the thick wood where not
a leaf stirred in the still, sultry air, and made his way
through the formal gardens without seeing so much as a
single rose, he told himself that if such as she had been

caring for the twins, it was no wonder that they were forward, pert, and disobedient. They were not children anymore; such behavior was unseemly in the extreme for my Ladies Anne and Amelia Fairhaven, the daughters of a duke of the realm.

He handed his hat to his smiling, bowing butler, and ordered, "A cool drink in the library at once, Devett, and then be so good as to ask Mrs. Pomfret to join me there immediately."

As he moved through the huge, cool hall, he said over his shoulder, "I have dismissed my daughters' governess. See that her trunks are packed and engage a seat for her on the next stage. I want her off the estate as soon as possible."

Devett so far forgot himself as to stare, and his mouth dropped open in amazement. One of the older footmen confided later to his cronies that he had never seen the like of it in all his born days.

"But—but, your Grace," the butler began. The slamming of the library door cut short any explanation he had been about to make.

Upstairs, the duke's daughters were helping each other to dress, and talking in excited whispers as they did so. Finally Amelia threw down the towel she had been using to dry Anne's hair and asked, "Why ever are we whispering, twin? There are two floors and acres of hallway between us and the Dreadful Duke. He cannot possibly hear us."

Her twin laughed and tossed her mane of thick black hair away from her face. "You are right, Melia. But I think we are still a little frightened. Did you see his face when he scolded Juliet? Brr!" She shivered a little as she sat down to pull on her stockings.

"How could I see?" Lady Amelia complained. "You kept pushing in front of me. But I did hear his cold angry voice, and that was quite enough for me." She joined her twin on the bench and reached for her own stockings, and then she sighed. "If only he had not come to Severn today, we might still be swimming, instead of dressing in these hot, confining clothes."

"Perhaps he won't stay long, Melia," Anne said. The elder by five minutes, she was much the braver of the two, and although her twin never hesitated to join her in whatever prank she was intent on at the moment, it was the Lady Anne who was the catalyst in all their adventures.

"He will stay long enough to learn that Miss Goffers has left and that Mr. Harden's shed burned down," Lady Amelia pointed out, rolling her stocking around her garter and pulling it smooth.

"But maybe no one will think to mention we were seen down in the village last week after midnight," Anne said, trying to look on the bright side of things. "And after all, he never stays at Severn long."

Lady Amelia stood up to fasten her petticoat. "Sometimes I wish he would, even as horrid as he is," she mused. "It is so quiet and lonesome here now the boys are gone."

"What fustian!" Anne exclaimed. "Why, if he stayed he would cut up all our peace, hedging us about and expecting us to be very pattern cards of propriety. We shall do very well without him; we always have."

Her voice was careless, but as her twin glanced at her face, she saw how pale it was with emotion. Anne wanted her father home as much as her twin did, but she would never admit it. Wisely, Amelia did not point out this obvious fact as she picked up a hairbrush to do her sister's hair.

"It is not quite dry, Anne," she said. "Perhaps we should braid it?"

The two girls, beside being identical in looks, always spoke of themselves as if they were one person. In addition, they finished each other's sentences, and were able to converse with only a glance. It was most unnerving for the other people who had to deal with them.

Now Anne gathered up her hair and piled it on her head, turning this way and that before the pier glass. "I wonder what we will look like when we are older and can wear it up?" she mused.

Amelia laughed. "Silly! I wish we had hair like Juliet's, so soft and pretty with all those golden strands in it. We look like two crows whether it is up or down."

The two studied themselves as they stood side by side. Besides a wealth of thick, wavy black hair, they had their father's soaring brows and aristocratic features. From their mother had come the deep-blue eyes and pale white skin. They were not at all the peaches-and-cream type of beauty they yearned to be so fervently, and at thirteen had no graceful curves. Instead, they seemed to be made up of sharp angles, all elbows and knees and narrow shoulder blades. They thought themselves ugly, but as Anne had pointed out, it really didn't make any difference what they looked like. As daughters of the Duke of Severn, their matrimonial futures were assured.

Now Anne shook her head sadly. "You're right, twin. We will never be beauties, will we?"

Lady Amelia shook her head. "No, but Juliet isn't a real beauty either, not like that Mrs. Kingley who came to see Father once. And remember, Anne, Juliet says that looks are not important and that a clever woman can make herself seem beautiful by her manners and wit and conversation."

"But we have no manners or wit or conversation," Anne argued, and then a knock came at the door. The little housemaid who told them their father wished to see them in the library seemed as frightened as they were, for her eyes were wide and she twisted her apron in nervous hands.

"Thank you, Betty," Lady Anne said, braiding her sister's hair as quickly as she could.

"We will be there directly," Lady Amelia added, her voice shaking now in fearful anticipation of the scene that was to come.

Two flights below, the duke was interviewing his housekeeper. Mrs. Pomfret, a tall, imposing figure clad in a black dress with her keys of office at her waist, stood quietly while her master explained the dismissal of his daughters' governess. Unlike the butler, she did not try to interrupt until the duke had finished.

"Your pardon, your Grace, but you are mistaken," she said then, her words slow and measured. "The young ladies have no governess at the present time. They have not had one since Miss Goffers left in a pet a month ago."

The duke lowered his mug of ale, and his black brows drew together in a frown. "Then, who was that unsuitable, brazen female I spoke to who was bathing with them in the lake?"

"I have no idea, your Grace," Mrs. Pomfret admitted, looking puzzled. "They were in the lake? Bathing?"

The duke nodded. "Almost completely unclothed, Mrs. Pomfret," he said grimly.

The housekeeper's thin lips tightened and she looked shocked.

"I see that I have more to do here than I thought," the duke remarked. "The escapades that my agent told me about were bad enough, but for my daughters, in the company of heaven knows what kind of depraved female, to be cavorting in their shifts in Severn's lake is such outrageous behavior that I am stunned."

"Should you like me to try to find out who the, er, the woman was, sir?" Mrs. Pomfret asked.

The duke waved his hand. "That will not be

necessary. I have asked the Ladies Anne and Amelia to attend me here. I am sure to get that information from them, after, of course, they have explained what on earth they thought they were doing to be in the lake in the first place."

Mrs. Pomfret stood with her hands folded quietly before her, her eyes lowered. It was a hot day, even here in the dim, high-ceilinged room of Severn, and for a moment she tried to imagine how refreshing the cool lake water must have felt. The duke's sarcastic tones recalled her to the problem at hand.

"That will be all for now, Mrs. Pomfret," he said in dismissal. "In the next few days, you and I will have a long talk about my daughters. I am not pleased with the way they are growing up, not pleased at all. I shall remain at Severn until the necessary corrections are made and they are brought to understand and conform to the exalted position they occupy."

Mrs. Pomfret curtsied, but as she rustled to the door, she thought, And what do even *you* think you can do with those limbs of Satan now, you who have all but ignored their existence from the day they were born?

It was only a few minutes later that Lady Anne and Lady Amelia knocked and entered the library. The duke watched them through narrowed eyes as they advanced toward him, hand in hand. They had grown taller since the last time he had seen them, but their slim figures, now covered with demure sprigged muslin gowns, long white stockings, and matching sandals, were still childish. He saw that they were wearing their hair tightly braided, and it made them appear even younger than they were.

As they curtsied, he continued to stare at them without speaking. The one on the left—Anne? Amelia?—stared back at him, while her twin lowered her eyes to the floor.

The bolder one began to speak, and then she had to

clear her throat when nothing but a croak emerged from her lips. He saw her white face pale even more, and knew she was embarrassed by her gaffe.

"Good afternoon, Father," she managed to get out at last. Her twin echoed her words only a second later.

"Sit down," the duke ordered, pointing to the two chairs that faced his desk. The girls did as they were bade quickly and without further comment.

"Now," he said, staring from one to the other. "Which is which?"

"I'm Anne." "I'm Amelia," came their reply, in unison again.

"Very well, Amelia," the duke continued, fixing the young lady in the right-hand chair with intent dark eyes. Lady Amelia concentrated on not cringing as he said, "Perhaps you will be so good as to give me an explanation of your behavior this afternoon?"

"Our behavior?" Lady Amelia asked, darting a glance at her twin as if begging for help.

"I am most displeased," the duke said. "Here I arrive at Severn to discover my daughters as good as naked in the lake, in full view of my coachman, grooms, and valet, or any other Tom, Dick, or Harry who might have come along. I would like an explanation, and at once."

"We did not know we would be in full view, and the gates are always locked. How could any Tom, Dick, or Harry come along?" Anne spoke up, trying to help her twin.

"I am speaking to your sister, young lady. You will be silent," the duke informed her, his voice cold.

Lady Anne subsided, sending a silent message to her twin.

"We did not expect you, your Grace," Lady Amelia whispered.

"That is obvious. But whether I am expected or not has nothing to do with the matter. I demand proper

27

conduct from my daughters at all times. What you did this afternoon was not only unbecoming to young ladies of your station, it was an indication of loose, careless immorality. You are not two little scullery maids, you know. You are the daughters of the Duke of Severn, and I'll thank you to remember it."

Although the duke's voice had not risen during this diatribe, both girls felt as if they had been scalded by his drawling, sarcastic lecture.

"Now, Lady Anne," their father said, turning toward her. He noticed that unlike her sister, this twin lifted her chin almost in defiance. It did not improve his mood. "I should like to hear any explanation you might have."

"It was so very hot, your Grace," she began. "And truly we did not expect anyone to come along. We are— we are very sorry, aren't we, Melia?"

The other twin nodded eagerly, and then she lowered her eyes to where she was clasping her hands in her lap at the cold, unforgiving light that burned in her father's eyes.

"And who was the woman who was with you?" the duke asked next.

"You don't know?" "But you talked to her for such a long time!" they said together.

"The length of my discussion with the woman has no bearing on the matter. I want her name, and I want to know what she was doing on the grounds."

"She is the Lady Juliet Manchester," Amelia whispered.

"The vicar's sister," Anne volunteered.

For a long moment there was silence in the library, and the twins stole a glance at their suddenly speechless father. He looked stunned and he seemed to have gone very far away. They could not know he was recalling some of the things he had said to the lady, and the accusations he had made. The words *wanton jade*

28

seemed to echo in his mind, and he almost groaned aloud.

"And what was the Lady Juliet Manchester, sister of the vicar, doing in Severn's lake?" he asked when he found his voice again.

"Bathing," Lady Amelia said in a little voice.

The duke leaned on his desk to glare at her. "You will contrive not to state the obvious to me, Amelia. I am not in the least slow-witted. I know she was bathing. I saw her doing so. I want to know why."

"Because it was so hot, of course," Anne interrupted again when her twin seemed to have lost her voice. She squirmed in her chair, absently scratching her arm as she did so, and willing her father to look at her and stop distressing Melia.

"What on earth do you think you are doing?" the duke inquired, staring at her scratching hand.

"It's this scab, sir," Anne told him, looking bewildered at his dark frown. "Something bit me and it itches."

"Stop that at once, you repellant child," her father said coldly. "Have you no notion at all of how you should comport yourself? Ladies do not scratch themselves in company. I am disgusted at the depth of your ignorance of polite behavior and ladylike conduct. You will leave me and go to your rooms. I have a great many plans to make in regard to you both, and I can see I must not waste a minute formulating those plans."

As the twins rose hastily and curtsied, he ran a hand over his dark hair and muttered, "If only I have not left it far too late!"

3

Although the Lady Juliet Manchester told her brother at dinner that evening of her meeting with the Duke of Severn, she did not feel it necessary to mention the state of undress she had been in at the time. Not, she thought, returning his sunny smile as she served him from the platter the maid was holding, that Romeo would be at all distressed by it. Indeed, with his good nature and appreciation of the ridiculous, he would probably laugh at her predicament until he was weak.

But the Lady Juliet was still feeling a little bruised by the duke's assessment of her as a wanton, ill-bred woman. And so, although she described his person, his dress, and demeanor to her brother, she did not reveal how angry he had been to discover her swimming in his lake, nor a word that he had said to her.

"I do not think I find the duke at all amiable, my dear," she said. "He appears to be a cold man, full of conceit and pride."

The vicar shook his head. "Pity, that," he remarked as he cut his veal. "There are so few of the gentry in this part of Devon."

His good-natured face creased in an unusual frown. "For your sake, Juliet, I wish he was a more gregarious type of fellow, given to having large house parties and entertainments. I am afraid you must be lonesome here, and bored."

His sister patted his hand. "I have not been bored in the least," she reassured him. "And the air in England is so refreshing after the heat of the American South."

Before her brother could continue to bemoan her quiet life, she changed the subject. Romeo was a dear brother and she loved him very much, but he tended to belabor a point, never willing to leave it until every ramification of it had been explored.

The next morning, he left early to drive to Barnstaple to visit an old friend from Oxford, a trip he made on the average of once a month. Juliet had toyed with the idea of accompanying him and doing some shopping, but since she was almost positive she was to have a morning caller, she did not hesitate to decline the journey.

It was another hot, sunny day, and she tied on a large Leghorn hat before she went out into the garden. There were some deadheads to be clipped, and she wanted to pick a bouquet for the vicarage parlor.

For a while she worked steadily, humming a little song as she pulled weeds in the bed of perennials. Faintly she could hear the cook's voice in the distance and the answering chatter of the maid, but here in the garden all was quiet and peaceful, with only the drone of the bees and an occasional trill of birdsong to keep her company.

It was almost eleven before the maid came out to find her. Her eyes were wide as she said, "Milady! The Duke of Severn has called and asked to see you."

Lady Juliet settled back on her heels, the trowel still in her hand.

"You may bring him out here, Phyllis," she said.

"Out here, milady?" the awed maid asked in some doubt.

Juliet could see she thought the parlor much more suitable for one of the duke's exalted stature, and she was sure the duke would be the first to agree with her.

"Please bring him to the garden, Phyllis," she said, glad she had a way to depress his pretensions. "And then I think a glass of my brother's sherry would be welcome. Did he walk down from the hall?" she asked, bending to uproot another weed.

The maid looked shocked. "Of course not, milady. Rode a horse, he did."

Juliet thought she sounded disappointed, almost as if she wished the duke had come in his state coach with numerous outriders all dressed in gold livery. She waved a dismissive hand and, as the maid left her, looked down at her white muslin morning gown.

She knew it was attractive. She had bought it in New Orleans, right off a ship from France. The tight bodice was banded with embroidered inserts of tiny pink roses, and the double flounces at the hem were trimmed in matching bands. Her wide-brimmed white hat sported a pink satin ribbon that tied under her chin.

Now she rose and stripped off her gardening gloves, setting them in a shallow basket with her trowel and secateurs, before she moved toward a pair of wicker chairs under the shade of a gnarled old apple tree.

When the duke appeared, he bowed to her, but he did not speak until the maid had disappeared.

"Lady Juliet Manchester?" he asked in the cool drawl she remembered.

Juliet nodded, inspecting him carefully now she was so close to him. What she saw made her heart beat a little faster, a reaction she was sure she shared with every woman who had ever met him. He was a handsome man, this Duke of Severn, and there was that about him that reminded you constantly of his masculinity and power.

"So, you discovered my name after all, your Grace," she said with a smile as she held out her hand. "And after telling me it was a matter of supreme indifference to you, too. But I am forgetting my manners. Won't you be seated?"

The duke nodded as he took the chair she indicated, but she thought he looked a little disconcerted at her words.

"I have come especially to apologize to you, ma'am,

for those words and some others I believe I used," he said, his dark eyes never leaving her face. "I had no idea who you were, and I am afraid I was less than, er, civil at our meeting."

Lady Juliet inclined her head. She was beginning to enjoy herself a great deal. The duke's voice had been tight and constrained, as if the apology had been a difficult one for him to make.

"I must admit I agree with you," she told him now. "You were uncivil to an extreme. But I am perfectly willing to forgive you. No doubt you were cross from the heat of the day and the dust of the road."

"And from seeing my daughters displaying themselves in such an immodest way," the duke could not refrain from remarking. "I was profoundly shocked."

Juliet was not forced to answer immediately, for Phyllis came back then with a decanter and glasses on a silver tray. Until the duke had been served, she was able to ponder how she was to handle this barely veiled suggestion that he had found her behavior profoundly shocking as well.

"You must remember that they are little more than children, your Grace," she said when they were alone again. "And the temptation of that beautiful lake right before their eyes on such a hot, sticky day was obviously too much for them to withstand."

"I am surprised you were a party to the prank even so, ma'am," he remarked, his voice even.

Lady Juliet felt her color rising. "Perhaps I had better explain exactly what happened, sir," she said. At his nod, she continued, "I had walked up to the hall to see the twins, as has become my custom once or twice a week. As I came around the bend in the drive, I found them already in the water. When I questioned them, I discovered that neither of them could swim more than a stroke or two. I was worried about them. If they had gone beyond their depth, or had a cramp, they might

33

have panicked, perhaps even drowned. And so I quickly removed my clothes and joined them."

"It was too good of you, m'lady," the duke said coldly. "But why didn't you merely order them to leave the water at once?"

"I, your Grace?" his hostess asked, her eyes wide. The duke saw they were an arresting shade of hazel, and thickly lashed. "But why on earth would they obey me? I have no authority over them. They would have laughed at the very idea."

At the duke's sudden frown, she added, "It is never good practice to *order* the young to do anything, for what you forbid them to do immediately becomes the most entrancing pastime in the world. With young girls, it is much better to gain your ends by devious means."

"I cannot agree with you there, ma'am," the duke said firmly. "I have given them a great many orders already, which I expect to be obeyed without question."

"Oh, dear, I am afraid that will not serve, sir," the lady said. "They will find some way to circumvent your commands, never fear."

"They had better not," the duke snapped, sounding like a man who was being pushed past his limit of patience. "But how can you know how they will behave? You are married with children of your own, perhaps? You do not appear to be old enough, unless you were wed at a very early age."

Lady Juliet turned aside for a moment when she felt her face stiffening. It was several moments before she had regained enough command over her voice and expression to say evenly, "I am one and thirty, your Grace, and no, I have never been married. But I have been a girl myself and, as such, have some knowledge of the behavior of my sex. Your daughters are typical. Tell them that they must on no account do a thing, and they will rush headlong into the completion of it, no matter how unsuitable it might be."

34

"But they are only thirteen! How dare they disobey their elders?" the duke exclaimed, so angered that for once his customary sarcastic drawl was missing.

"I do assure you Grace that age has nothing to do with it. And thirteen is quite old enough for the female sex to be up to a great deal of mischief," Lady Juliet remarked, her voice calm and steady. "And then it is true that your daughters are precocious. I have often felt it was a shame that they were twins."

"Why?" he asked, unable to follow her line of reasoning.

"Because they encourage each other to wilder and wilder escapades. If there were only one, there would be no such behavior. As it is, what Anne suggests, Amelia embellishes, and before you know what they are about, they are deep in trouble and everything is topsy-turvy."

"Including my peace," he growled, running a hand over his smooth dark hair in frustration.

Lady Juliet smiled a little. "Well, you can always go away again, and then your peace will be restored," she pointed out.

"I have no intention of going away until I have brought the girls to a proper concern for their conduct and manners," he told her grimly.

"Then we may all look forward to having you grace the neighborhood for some time to come, I see," Lady Juliet said. "I fear you will have a formidable time of it, but I am glad that you plan to undertake the task. Your daughters need the supervision that a housekeeper or governess cannot give, even with the best of intentions. Besides, Anne and Amelia have been lonely since their brothers went away. Severn is much too palatial and formal for two young girls left only with an army of servants."

She paused, wondering if she had said too much, but the duke was stroking his chin, deep in thought.

"They have been fortunate to have had your friendship, then, ma'am," he said more mildly. "I do not recall your being here when I was last at Severn. You have only recently arrived?"

"I came to live with my brother a year ago, your Grace. Before that I lived abroad in North America for many years."

She stopped abruptly, and the duke leaned forward in his chair, putting his wineglass down on the table beside him. "Where?" he asked.

He seemed interested, and Lady Juliet forced herself to say, "In Louisiana, your Grace. That is a part of the Louisiana Purchase you might know of, bordering the Gulf of Mexico."

"I know it well, for I have been there myself," he replied. "But I must say I am surprised. I should think that a dangerous part of the world for an English-woman. I was there a few years ago, and I found that most Americans have a great hatred for the British. Understandable, of course, when you consider impress-ment gangs and the embargoes that ruined their trade and strangled their commerce."

"Yes, it was not very comfortable at times," Lady Juliet said slowly, her eyes far away. The duke was watching her keenly, but she did not seem to notice. "After my father's death when I was twenty, my mother and I went to live with her sister, who had married a French plantation owner. At Bellemanoir my mother was content until she contracted typhoid and died two years ago. When war was declared, I decided to leave. As an Englishwoman, I was an embarrassment to my relatives, and there was no reason for me to remain any longer."

She paused for a moment and the duke saw how she was clenching her hands together in her lap. Then she took a deep breath and released her fingers as she said lightly, "But there is nothing more boring than being treated to an account of another's travels. Suffice it to say, I am delighted to be home. Even the heat of Devon cannot compare to the sultry, humid summers of southern America."

The duke saw that she had retreated again behind a mask of politeness, almost as if she feared she had said too much. He rose and bowed.

"I have taken too much of your time, m'lady, but perhaps we can continue our discussion some other day? I did not find it at all boring. Indeed, as any of my friends could tell you, although I am easily bored, I am quick to call the matter to the offender's attention."

Juliet smiled at him, willing herself to put the dark memories behind her as she had done so many times before.

"Thank you for accepting my apologies, m'lady," the duke was saying now. "I was sorry to miss the vicar, but I understand he has gone to Barnstaple today. Do say everything that is proper for me. I shall make it a point to call on him in the near future."

Juliet rose too at his return to his usual sarcastic drawl. She noticed that although she was not at all a little dab of a woman, she was much shorter than the duke. In fact, the top of her head did not quite reach his shoulder. From his great height, the dark duke looked down at her with hooded eyes. For some reason, the little flutter she felt in the region of her heart made her angry. She was not an impressionable girl whose head could be turned in an instant, no matter how handsome and sophisticated the man. Her own expression grew cool as she gave him a deep curtsy.

"I am sure my brother will be honored and delighted," she said.

The duke looked at her sharply. Her words had been conventional and spoken in a demure voice, but there was something there that made him stiffen. Did she think him condescending? Was she trying to put him in his place?

"Allow me to show you out, your Grace," she said, picking up her skirts to lead the way from the garden. "There is a gate to the stables through here. You rode down from Severn, did you not?"

The duke decided to ignore her earlier remark. "Yes. As you remarked, it is much too hot and sultry to walk, even this early in the day."

As they reached the gate, she paused and held out her hand. "Thank you for calling, your Grace," she said. Her voice was even and devoid of any nuances now, and she favored him with a smile.

The duke admired those glowing hazel eyes and even white teeth, and then his eyes strayed to the little mole beside her mouth. Without thinking of what he was doing, he reached out and touched it gently with one powerful finger. Juliet did not move, but her smile faded and she looked almost frightened. Idly, the duke wondered why.

"I have often wondered what our ancestors of both sexes looked like wearing their beauty patches and dressed for a ball," he mused. "And here you have a permanent one. It is charming."

Juliet could think of nothing to say in reply to this gallantry.

"Did you know the various patches all had different names, ma'am?" he asked. She shook her head. "That one placed beside the mouth was called 'The Kissing.' Appropriate, was it not?"

He had bent a little closer as he spoke, and Juliet took a deep breath and stepped away. He smiled down at her for a moment before he bowed again and went away, feeling better for some reason that he had the last word.

Juliet went back to the flower beds, but somehow she found herself thinking of the duke and remembering his words, and the remaining weeds continued to flourish.

The Duke of Severn—proud, conceited, and all too well aware of his omnipotence and desirability—was still an attractive, dangerous man, even to some one as cool to the male sex as Lady Juliet Manchester. She remembered that he had asked if she were married with children of her own, and how she had stiffened at the question and had been forced to turn aside until she had control over her voice and expression once again. Her spinsterhood was none of his business. Let him think of her as he wished, she had no intention of explaining the circumstances that had brought her to the advanced age of one and thirty while still unwed.

She was recalled to the present when she heard a sibilant *psst!* from behind the garden wall, and she rose from her knees and called, "Yes? Who is there?"

"Has he gone?" a little voice asked in a desperate whisper.

"*Really* gone?" another voice added.

Lady Juliet smiled and, speaking in her normal voice, said, "Yes, the duke has departed. You are quite safe."

Two black heads appeared over the top of the wall, and then the twins pulled themselves up and over to drop on the grass below, exposing what seemed to be yards of white petticoats and frilled drawers as they did so.

"Why ever didn't you walk around to the gate?" Lady Juliet asked in some amusement.

"We can stay only a little while," Lady Anne said, running to her side to hug and kiss her.

"We have to be at the hall for luncheon at one, and we dare not be late," Lady Amelia told her, kissing her other cheek.

The lady put an arm around them both. "Now, what is this desperate visit all about?" she asked, dropping down on the sunlit grass and motioning them to follow her.

"It is Father, of course," Lady Anne said, her thin face serious and the black brows so like the duke's in an identical frown. "Oh, it is terrible, Juliet! You would not believe the things he has insisted we do. We might just as well be prisoners in a dungeon," she ended in a wail.

Her twin patted her hand. "Indeed, it is too bad, m'lady," this one added more mildly. "We are expected to spend the morning with our books, and without a governess to help us, mind you. Then we have to sit in that huge formal dining room surrounded by footmen and all manner of pomp and ceremony for every meal. The duke says our table manners leave a lot to be desired."

"And we are not to ride astride anymore, or go anywhere, even in the grounds, without a groom in attendance," Lady Anne said, continuing the list of grievances, and then she added darkly, "Why, we are not even allowed to scratch when we itch! Did you ever hear of such a thing?"

Lady Juliet swallowed the bubble of laughter that threatened to disgrace her with her young friends.

"That does sound rather extreme," she said when she was able to speak, "but I am sure the duke feels all these restrictions are for your own good."

"Huh!" Lady Anne exclaimed, tossing her long black hair. "*He* does not care for us, he never has. It is all so we won't embarrass *him,* disgrace *him* when we are old enough to go out in company."

"Uphold all *his* fusty old-fashioned ideas of propriety, grow up to be worthy of *him,*" Lady Amelia concluded.

Anne jumped to her feet and struck a pose. "You are not two little scullery maids, and I'll thank you to remember it," she pronounced in her deepest, most scornful voice while she sneered, her nose in the air.

"Oh, dear," Lady Juliet said weakly. "He did not really say that, did he?"

"That and much, much more," Lady Amelia said in

a voice full of doom. She plucked a nearby daisy and began to strip it of its petals with shaking fingers. "How silly! We know we are not two scullery maids!"

"What are we going to do, Juliet?" Lady Anne asked, her hands still on her hips. "You can see that the situation is—is intolable."

"Intolerable," Lady Juliet corrected her absently.

Both girls repeated the word together, and then they waited quietly for their friend to solve their problem.

The church clock rang the half-hour, and she rose and shook out her skirts. "What you must do right now is run back to the hall, so as not to be late for luncheon," she said. "I will consider what you have told me, and perhaps I can find a way to help. In the meantime, try to do what the duke orders. It is too bad, of course, but he is your father. And if you seem to be conforming to his wishes, he may not stay at Severn long."

Lady Amelia shook her head as she rose to join her twin. "I am afraid he is here for a long stay. I heard him ordering his valet to send to London for a more extensive wardrobe."

"And we will miss our drive to the seashore, Juliet," Lady Anne told her. "You know that we planned to go tomorrow if the weather continues fine."

"I see no reason why the three of us cannot do that even now," Juliet said soothingly as she walked with them to the postern gate that led into the churchyard and then into Severn's park beyond. "I shall write a note to the duke inviting you to join me. Why wouldn't he be agreeable to such a jaunt? You will be in my care, after all."

The two girls' faces lit up in identical smiles. "That's famous," Anne exclaimed, while Amelia hugged their friend, content for once to let her twin speak for them both.

But when Lady Juliet penned a note to the duke later

that afternoon, asking his permission to take his daughters to the coast, the reply that arrived so swiftly denied them the treat.

"I thank you for your kindness, m'lady," the duke wrote in a slashing black hand as powerful-looking as he was himself, "but amusements for the Ladies Anne and Amelia cannot be permitted at this time. Perhaps at a later date?"

He had signed it "Severn," and then had added a postscript. "I would not have a moment's peace all afternoon. If they succumbed so swiftly to the lure of Severn's lake, what might they not do when presented with the vast Atlantic Ocean?"

Juliet was torn between laughter and chagrin. She found herself hoping that the twins would behave themselves and that the duke would mellow in regard to his daughters. They were wonderful girls, clever and intelligent, with sparkling personalities, and she hated to think that they might be forced into a rigid mold of strict propriety, afraid to laugh or enjoy life for fear of breaking one of society's fusty rules. It really was too bad that their mother had died at their birth, she thought, one finger absently tracing the bold letters of his title. Since the duke had never married again, he must have loved her very much, and surely she would have been able to temper his inflexible notions about the correct way to rear a child.

4

There was no traffic between Severn and the manse in the next few days. Juliet pondered walking up to the hall to inquire for the young ladies, but something seemed to tell her that such a visit would be most unwise. And although she had smiled at the duke's reply to her invitation to his daughters, now she could not help wondering if perhaps he still considered her an unfit companion for them. After all, she had shocked him by joining them in the lake, and even though he knew why she had done so, and had apologized for the names he had called her, might he still not consider her a wanton jade, the type of woman who must be kept away from them at all costs? Her eyes grew bitter for a moment and her lips tightened, and then she made herself think of other things.

And so she went about her duties at the manse, working outside on fine days in the garden she had taken as her own special charge, and occupying herself with her sewing when it began to rain.

The rain broke the heat spell they had been suffering, and the following morning dawned bright and much cooler. It was Sunday, and as Juliet dressed for church, she wondered if All Saints would be honored that day by the duke and his daughters gracing the elaborate Severn pew that was set apart from the others, directly beneath the lectern?

She had invited the girls to come with her many times after she discovered they had lost the habit of regular churchgoing, but this Sunday she sent no message to the hall. The duke might see to his daughters' religious instruction if he chose to do so; it was no longer any of her concern.

Juliet was surprised to find how much she missed her meetings with Anne and Amelia. Her brother had spoken truly when he said there was little in the way of amusements for her to enjoy, and their bright chatter and gay spirits had enlivened many a long afternoon.

She took her seat in the old stone church with its beautiful stained-glass windows after greeting those of the villagers who had arrived even earlier than she, and began to read her prayer book. Not many moments passed before the rustling and whispers behind her told her even without looking that the duke and his family had made an appearance after all. As they passed her pew, she turned to smile at the twins. To her surprise, they marched right by her, eyes straight ahead. They were wearing white dresses with blue velvet sashes, and on their heads flat-crowned straw hats trimmed with matching blue ribbon that trailed down their narrow backs. Behind them, in faultless morning dress came the duke, his tall beaver in his gloved hand.

Her eyebrows rose a little, and then the duke glanced sideways and gave her a small smile as if to say, "See, it only required a little resolution on my part to turn them into perfect paragons."

Juliet lowered her eyes to her prayer book, not at all convinced. There had been a definite mulish cast to Anne's tight lips and Amelia had not looked completely cowed either.

She was glad her brother's sermon was so timely. He took his text from St. Matthew, preaching on the kingdom of heaven and including the fourteenth verse of Chapter Nineteen, which instructed the disciples to "suffer the little children to come unto me." Juliet said a prayer that the duke would remember that his daughters, although thirteen now, were not far removed from childhood themselves.

As she made her way down the aisle at the conclusion of the service, she was delayed by one of the women from the village. Her mother was ill and she begged Lady Juliet to call. By the time the date had been arranged and the hour set, the church was almost empty and the party from Severn had disappeared. Juliet felt a pang of regret. She would have liked to speak to the twins, to find out for herself how they were coming along.

She reached her brother's side where he stood at the church door to greet his flock, and she waited for him there until he was ready to return to the manse. As they strolled through the churchyard, he still wearing his white surplice and carrying his Bible, he said, "I have wonderful news, my dear! We have been invited to dinner at the hall this coming Wednesday evening. The duke was most pleasant, most agreeable. And now you will be able to wear one of your fine gowns and enjoy a civilized conversation."

Juliet laughed and squeezed his arm. "As if you and I did not have intelligent conversations every day of the week, Romeo. But I am glad of the invitation. I must find out how the twins are surviving this new and strict regime."

"Perhaps the duke will invite others of his friends," her brother continued. From his eager tone of voice, his sister knew he was hoping she would meet some suitable, single gentleman, and she sighed inwardly. Even though the vicar had never married and had confessed that he felt no urge to do so, he had not given up hoping that his younger sister might even now attain that blessed state. Juliet shook her head. She had never told her brother why such a course was impossible for her, and even more unattractive to her than it appeared to be to him. She could not tell even him the secret she kept locked so tightly in her heart.

Now she was quick to compliment him on his sermon

45

and pass on all the village news she had heard that morning, to distract him from her regrettable, to him, single state.

Juliet's patience was sorely tested for the next three days. Her brother could not seem to stop talking of the dinner invitation and the possibilities it presented. In vain, Juliet reminded him that the duke was only being courteous in inviting his vicar and his sister to the hall, and that as soon as this duty had been accomplished, they would in all probability see him no more.

The Reverend Manchester was a confirmed optimist, however, and his hazel eyes, so like his sister's, gleamed with anticipation behind his spectacles as he enumerated the picnic parties, balls, and teas they were sure to be invited to as a result of the duke's continued residency.

The duke had arranged for his carriage to collect them on Wednesday evening, and the vicar was ready well before time. Juliet found him peering out the window when she came down at last, pulling on her long white gloves as she did so.

He turned to inspect her, and then he rubbed his hands together and smiled. "How lovely you look, Juliet," he told her, his voice full of admiration.

Juliet gave him a mock curtsy. She was wearing a silk gown of lime green that complimented her eyes. Her maid had wanted to dress her hair in clusters of curls, but Juliet had insisted on her usual soft chignon. It was secured with a deeper-green satin ribbon that matched the trimming of the low, round neckline. At her throat and wrists she wore her mother's pearls, and draped over her arms was a gossamer shawl covered with delicate embroidery. It was another of her gowns from France, and she knew that even if the duke had invited a bevy of smart London ladies, they would all be envious of her turnout. Since Napoleon had closed the French capital to Englishwomen, they were forced to depend on local dressmakers, instead of the talented Parisian modistes.

This thought allowed Juliet to enter Severn with her usual aplomb. But as they were announced and came into the drawing room arm in arm, she saw that they were the only guests. The duke was standing before the massive fireplace, dressed entirely in black evening clothes that were relieved only by the gleaming white of his waistcoat and cravat. Such was his presence, he was not a bit overshadowed by the elaborate room that rose some twenty feet to a gilded ceiling and was furnished with all manner of gilt furniture and rich brocades. As Juliet rose from her curtsy, she saw the Ladies Anne and Amelia flanking their father and looking identically mutinous.

The duke welcomed them in his slow, sarcastic drawl, and then he turned to his daughters.

"I know I do not have to make you known to the Ladies Anne and Amelia," he said, and Juliet saw how carefully he watched as the twins made their curtsies. Amelia stumbled a little and turned pale at the frown that came between her father's eyes.

Juliet went to give her a kiss and a quick hug to reassure her.

"Indeed you do not, your Grace," she said easily, smiling at the girls. "I am delighted to see them again, as is my brother. We have missed their visits, haven't we, Romeo?"

As the vicar was echoing this sentiment, a wicked little smile played over the duke's mouth. "But why have I never made the connection before?" he murmured, as if much amused. "Why, you are Romeo and Juliet!"

Lady Anne gave a little giggle, and he turned swiftly to glare at her, leaving her covered with confusion. Juliet longed to slap him.

"Our mother was romantic, your Grace," the vicar was saying now as he took the glass of wine the duke's butler was presenting. "That particular play of Shakespeare's was one of her favorites."

"Absurd, is it not?" Juliet asked with a special smile for Anne. "I can think of nothing more unsuitable than a clergyman named Romeo, especially since my brother has no interest in matrimony."

"Perhaps, as Juliet, you will fulfill her dreams," the duke remarked.

Juliet tried not to stiffen, and then she made herself smile a little before she turned once again to the twins. They had not spoken a word since the arrival of the guests, and this was so unlike them, Juliet was disturbed. "Sit with me and tell me what you have been doing, m'ladies," she invited, indicating a sofa a little distance from the duke.

She saw the twins look to their father for permission. At his little nod, they were quick to join her.

"We have been much involved in our studies," Lady Anne announced in a dead little voice.

"*Much* involved," Lady Amelia agreed, her voice discouraged.

"But surely you have been riding or walking in the park," Juliet persisted.

Anne squeezed her hand under cover of her dress. "Yes, Father is kind enough to take us for a ride every fine afternoon," she said.

"Sometimes we go for a drive in his phaeton," Lady Amelia added.

Juliet was growing very concerned. She felt she was in the company of two pale little ghosts. Oh, how she longed to tell this arrogant duke exactly what she thought of his methods of child rearing, she thought to herself. Whatever had he been doing to turn them into such wooden puppets? She would never have imagined

48

the girls' spirits could be broken so quickly. Was it possible that he had beaten them?

She watched them carefully, even as she kept up a light, artless chatter, and when the austere butler came to announce dinner, she was glad when Lady Amelia whispered as they rose together, "How we have missed you, dear Juliet," and Anne added, "We shall contrive some way to see you, never fear!"

Somewhat relieved, she allowed the duke to escort her to the dining salon, her brother extending a courteous arm to each of his young hostesses, and chatting gaily with them as he did so.

"Surely you must applaud my efforts, Lady Juliet," the duke murmured, bending his dark head closer to hers. "You can see how improved the twins are, even in this short time."

He sounded so smug that Juliet did not even try to temper her reply. "On the contrary, your Grace," she said, her voice cold, "I cannot applaud it. I find them vastly changed, as prim and lifeless as two little dolls. I must say I regret the loss of their former vivacity and charm."

The duke almost missed his step. "Indeed?" he asked, his voice rich with sarcasm. "In my viewpoint, until they have learned how to behave as titled young ladies, I do not care if they have an ounce of vivacious charm. We are not likely to agree on the subject. But why am I surprised at that? Since our first meeting I have been all too aware that our opinion of what constitutes correct behavior is very much at odds."

They were moving down a long corridor now, lined with paintings and glass cabinets filled with rare china and crystal. Juliet found herself growing steadily more angry, but she controlled herself and said sweetly, "Forgive me, your Grace, but I find you ridiculous. You must be aware that ladies in evening dress show much more of themselves than you were permitted to see when I was in the lake. Do you censor them for improper behavior?"

The duke's dark eyes slowly inspected the white skin of her shoulders and half-concealed bosom, and Juliet wished she had worn a gown with a more modest neckline. "Why, no, Lady Juliet," he drawled, his amused voice soft so only she might hear it. "I am too busy admiring the, er, the view. But what I enjoy and what is suitable for thirteen-year-old girls are two entirely different things."

"Is that why you do not permit the twins to see me anymore, sir?" she asked, her voice stiff. "I can assure you that mine is not a *corruptive* influence."

The duke looked a little disconcerted. "I beg your pardon, m'lady. Perhaps I spoke too hastily. No, the Ladies Anne and Amelia have been denied the pleasure of visiting you until such time as they have shown me they will obey me without question, behave properly at all times, and apply themselves diligently to their studies. The depth of their ignorance in almost every subject is appalling."

Somewhat appeased, Juliet let him lead her up to the table in the massive salon. The ceiling arched far above them, and between the massive pillars that lined the walls, every inch of space was covered by murals of classical subjects. The marble door cases were richly carved, the work of Grinling Gibbons, and further adorned by the duke's coat of arms set in arched recesses above the doors themselves. Behind every gilt chair, a footman in scarlet livery stood at attention, and more lined the walls.

The duke seated her at his right hand and indicated the vicar was to take the place at his left. The twins faced each other below them. All the chairs were set a distance apart from each other, and although Juliet was sure several leaves had been removed from the massive table, it was not at all a cozy setting. Conversation would of necessity have to be conducted in loud voices so everyone could hear.

The duke signaled his butler, and the footmen sprang into action. "Do you still enjoy life in Devon, sir?" he asked the vicar as one of the footmen spread a damask napkin reverently on his lap.

"Very much so, your Grace," Romeo told him, his eyes twinkling behind his spectacles. "Of course you know I have been vicar here some ten years. I find the climate salubrious and the inhabitants pleasant. If I have any regrets at all, it is the paucity of polite society in the neighborhood, especially since Juliet has come to live with me."

The duke turned to his right. "And do you also regret the lack of society, m'lady?" he asked.

Juliet was not fooled by his colorless words. She nodded to the footman presenting a tureen of bisque, and then she said, "I do not. I enjoy the quiet life here after the upheavals and alarums of America, but I cannot make my brother understand that I do not want a life gay with dissipation. He is still bemoaning the fact I would not go to London this past Season."

"London has suffered," the duke remarked, bowing a little in her direction.

Juliet applied herself to her soup. Beside her, Anne's spoon clattered against the rim of her bowl, and to cover the slip, Juliet said brightly, "How delicious the bisque is, your Grace. And do I detect prawns as well as lobster in the ingredients?"

The duke ignored his daughter, who was now delicately spooning her soup carefully into her mouth.

"I would not be surprised," he said. "My chef is noted for his seafood dishes. He is French, of course."

"So, you do not believe that because we are at war with France, you should dispense with a Frenchman's services?" Juliet asked.

The duke shrugged and then he sipped his wine. "I am not at war with François except when he sends up a dish that is less than perfect," he told her, and then he added, "But you are no one to be calling the kettle black, m'lady, not dressed as you are in a Parisian gown."

Juliet chuckled. *"Touché,* your Grace. It is true I bought most of my gowns in New Orleans, and that city, as you must be aware, does not suffer any lack of smart Parisian fashions."

The duke studied her gown, and then he said, "I detect the fine hand of Madame Odile, do I not?"

Lady Juliet nodded, and then she broke into a torrent of French. The duke's black eyes grew keener, and when she had finished with a very French shrug, he laughed and replied in the same language.

Lady Juliet looked around to see both girls staring at her in astonishment, and she said in English, "It is not at all kind of you to twit me on my French, your Grace. I realize that I owe more to the Cajuns of Louisiana for my pronunciation than any pure, Parisian accent, for it is the French I have heard spoken for many years."

"I protest, it is charming," the duke assured her. "That slow drawl, the twist of the syllables, charming!"

He smiled at his guest, and Lady Amelia stared at him, an arrested expression coming over her face. Then she turned to her twin, to find her looking back at her intently. The two girls sat motionless for a long moment, their eyes locked, and then a little smile curved their lips and they both nodded. It was obvious that m'ladies Anne and Amelia had come to the same lightning-fast conclusion, and it appeared to delight them both.

The duke suddenly remembered his daughters and looked down the table to where Amelia was sitting, ignoring her soup. "You do not seem to care for your dinner, Amelia. That is not polite. Please begin to eat it at once.''

Obediently, the girl picked up her spoon, and Lady Anne cried, ''Do not eat it, twin!'' At the duke's angry, astonished look, she added defiantly, ''Melia cannot eat shellfish. It makes her break out in spots. Large, red, *itchy* spots!''

The duke's frown became ferocious. ''That will be quite enough, Anne,'' he snapped. ''A dinner table is no place to discuss one's physical infirmities.''

He turned then to the Manchesters with a look that seemed to ask them what on earth he was to do with such inept, impossible creatures, but Juliet, who had been struck with a sudden idea, did not notice the appeal in his eyes.

Could it be possible? she wondered to herself. Surely she must be imagining it, for such devious maneuvering was surely beyond the ken of two young girls. She was brought back to the company when she heard the duke saying, ''Since you cannot eat your soup, Amelia, it might be appropriate for you to join in the conversation. What do you think of Lady Juliet's gown?''

''It—it is very beautiful, Fa—Father,'' she whispered.

''What? Speak up! No one can hear you,'' the duke commanded.

The tense silence seemed to go on forever, and then Lady Amelia almost shouted, ''I said it was very beautiful!''

Juliet was grateful when her brother began to speak, as if the situation was completely normal. ''And that is another thing, your Grace. What is the sense of all of Juliet's lovely gowns if she will not consent to go to town? M'aunt, the Marchioness of Hanover, has invited her repeatedly, but nothing I can say will change her mind.''

During this artless speech, the duke had regained control of himself, and now he said, "Strange. I do not care for the country myself and would never leave town at all unless I was forced to do so. I have several friends who adore it, of course, but I have never been able to fathom why. It is so quiet, so dull, so—so uninspiring."

"I like it," Lady Anne said defiantly, setting her soup spoon down in her bowl. The duke glared at it until she looked down, gasped, and quickly picked up the spoon to place it on the service plate.

Juliet was sure now that her earlier suspicion that the twins were deliberately baiting their father was true after all.

"I fear I must ask you to forgive my daughters, Reverend Manchester, m'lady," the duke said, his drawl annoyed. "They have much to learn about polite behavior, and we are finding it quite an uphill battle, are we not, twins?"

"Yes," both girls answered together.

Juliet thought they sounded not only amused, but triumphant. She found herself wanting very badly to laugh, and she made herself say, "I am positive that they will improve very quickly, your Grace. At their age, an occasional mistake is hardly world-shaking. By the time they make their come-outs, surely they will be the epitome of grace and good taste."

The duke bent a dark, incredulous eye on her. "But isn't it customary for girls to debut when they are eighteen, ma'am?" he asked. At Juliet's nod, he added, "Then we have only five years to accomplish such a miraculous transformation. I do not think, from my present assessment of the situation, that even ten would suffice."

Juliet took a serving of chicken, and nodded an assent to the footman offering the wine and mushroom sauce. She was torn between anger and amusement. The twins were behaving very badly, that was true, but it was unkind of the duke to discuss their faults in front of others.

Thinking to change the subject, she said, "Perhaps I will agree to go to London sometime this year, Romeo. I would like to see the new plays, the art exhibitions, and the opera. My education has been sadly neglected too, m'ladies," she added with a sideways smile. "All those years that I spend abroad have left me sadly behind the times."

Her brother was quick to applaud this plan, and he began to ask the duke about the current London scene. Under cover of the men's discussion, Juliet raised her napkin to her lips, and turning a little sideways, she said so only Anne could hear her, "Enough is enough, Anne. You can see how uncomfortable this is for the vicar—and for me."

She looked into the girl's eyes, expecting to see them filled with defiance, and was surprised to see her tiny nod of acquiescence. Knowing full well that Anne would communicate the cease-fire to her twin with only a glance, she applied herself to her dinner and the excellent wines the duke had arranged to be served.

Dinner became almost pleasant from that time on. The girls made no further mistakes in their table manners, and they even joined in the conversation without being prodded to do so. By the time dessert was served, the duke began to relax and enjoy himself. He studied Lady Juliet over the rim of his champagne glass. She was leaning forward, in answer to some question Amelia had put to her, and the candlelight glimmered on her white throat and shoulders and brought into bold relief the exciting curves of her swelling breasts. She had beautiful skin, the duke thought, as smooth and creamy as the pearls she wore. Her only blemish, although he did not consider it such, was the small mole beside her rosy mouth. Idly he wondered if perhaps the mole had a twin hidden somewhere out of sight, and he began to place it in locations that would please him most.

He managed to reply to the vicar's question about repairs to the paneling of one of the church chapels without pausing to consider the abrupt change of subject. At forty-two, the duke was certainly sophisticated enough to manage not only moles but mildew without missing a beat.

When the three ladies rose at the end of the meal to leave the gentlemen to their port, the duke himself came to help Lady Juliet from her chair. As he turned to his daughters, he wondered at their air of suppressed excitement. Anne was nodding, almost in approval, and Amelia gave him a shy smile. Beginning to know the twins as well as he did, he could not help feeling a little shiver of apprehension. What were they up to now?

5

The happy truce that was the state of affairs when the vicar and Lady Juliet left Severn that evening did not survive for very long. The duke, feeling that a great deal of progress had been made, asked his daughters to join him in the library early the next morning so he might give them his compliments.

Only the Lady Amelia appeared. She seemed a little distraught, and when he asked where Anne was, she blushed and stammered until his suspicions were aroused.

"Out with it, Amelia!" he ordered. "Where is Anne?"

"Why, she is in her room, Fa—Father," she said, her blue eyes wide. "She—she is not quite dressed."

The duke was forced to accept this excuse, and after he had told her he was very pleased with *most* of her behavior the evening before, he dismissed her, asking her to send Anne to him as soon as possible.

It was only a few minutes later that Anne knocked and slipped into the library. "You wished to see me, Father?" she asked, looking him straight in the eye. She was wearing a blue gown identical to her sister's, but the duke saw she had on a white sash, instead of a pink one Amelia had chosen. He was surprised, for he had never seen the twins when they were not dressed exactly alike, right down to the color of their hair ribbons.

He went through his congratulatory speech once again, and his daughter thanked him gravely. When he told her to return to her books, she curtsied and turned to leave. It was then that he saw the pink ribbons that were tied around her braids.

"Amelia!" he called out in a harsh voice, and she stopped short and turned back. Then her mouth formed a perfect O of guilt, and her hands went up to cover it in her chagrin at being caught out.

"Come here, Amelia," the duke ordered, his expression grim. The girl did as she was bade, but she looked as if she would rather be anywhere else on earth.

"Now you will tell me, and at once, why you are masquerading as your sister, young lady," he ordered, his dark eyes stern on her pale face. "Where is she? And no lies, if you know what is good for you."

"She went fishing," Lady Amelia said softly.

"Fishing?" the duke asked as if he had never heard of such a thing. "But she knows she is supposed to spend her mornings in study."

"But it is such a perfect day for fishing, Father. There is no wind, and it is slightly overcast," Amelia pointed out as if that made her twin's truancy more palatable.

She was deeply disappointed that they had been discovered, for if the weather continued the same, Anne had been going to cover for her on the morrow.

"Go to your room," the duke ordered coldly. "You will remain there until I tell you you may leave it. I trust I will not have to station a footman outside your door to make sure you obey me?"

Stung, Lady Amelia gave him a hurt look before she lowered her eyes again. "That will not be necessary, Father," she said, her voice stiff.

She started to leave, and the duke was struck by a sudden thought. "Have you played this trick on me before, Amelia?" he asked.

She looked up and saw he was determined to have an answer. "Yes, sir," she whispered. "Once or twice."

"Good Lord," he muttered, and then he added, "You act your sister very well." His daughter was not fooled by the compliment. "I would never have guessed, if you had not thought to embellish your performance."

"Em-, embellish it?" Amelia asked, a little frown coming between her brows.

"You, er, gilded the lily, my dear. You see, I have noticed that the two of you always dress exactly alike. Changing your sash to make yourself seem different was a major mistake."

Amelia's hand went to her sash, and he saw she was thinking hard. Suddenly she smiled. "Of course! And then you saw the pink ribbons in my hair, didn't you? How quick you are, Father!"

The duke ruined this budding sense of rapport by saying tartly, "I beg you will remember it in the future, Amelia, and try no further deceptions. You are excused."

He rose from his desk, and Amelia curtsied quickly and almost ran from the room.

The duke strolled to the French doors of the library

and looked down toward the lake. Not a ripple marred the water directly before him, but he knew Anne would never dare to fish in sight of the hall. Coming to a sudden decision, he nodded, and then he opened the doors and left the library.

It was almost half an hour before the duke found his delinquent daughter. He had started walking quickly around the lake, even though he knew it was entirely possible that Anne was fishing one of the trout streams instead. And then, as he came to the end of the lake, he saw her. She was seated in a punt, some distance from shore, and as he watched, she cast her line with an expert flick of her rod. He marched down to the bank and was about to call to her when she had a strike. The pole dipped suddenly and the line grew taut, and then the punt began to move. He was struck by a sudden fear, remembering what the Lady Juliet had told him about his daughters' almost nonexistent ability to swim, and without thinking he stripped off his jacket and sat down to remove his boots. He never took his eyes from the slim figure who was trying to reel in her catch, and crowing as she did so. The line must have snagged on some underwater obstruction, for Anne got to her feet to try to free it.

"Sit down, you little fool," the duke muttered, tugging at his boot, his eyes intent on her struggles.

And then, as if in slow motion, what he had been dreading occurred. The line snapped, the punt slid sideways, and Lady Anne tumbled into the water. The duke ran to the lake and waded in until it was deep enough for him to dive forward and began a fast stroke, the trudgen he had learned a few years before. He looked up only once and was glad to see Anne had had the presence of mind to grasp the gunwale of the punt when she surfaced. He relaxed his pace a little to call out, "Hang on, Anne! I'm coming!"

He saw her eyes widen with relief when she realized

she was not alone, and the little nod she gave to tell him she understood. He was beside her in a few moments, wrapping one strong arm around her waist and turning her on her back. She tried to put her arms around his neck, and he said harshly, "Lie still! I cannot tow you to shore if you fight me."

He could feel her trembling and he said more gently, "You are all right now, my dear. I have you safe."

As soon as he felt her tense muscles relax, he began a slow sidestroke to the shallows. He could hear her gasping and sobbing, and he hugged her closer. "Shhh," he said. "Nothing will happen to you now, my promise on it."

When they reached the shore, he stood her up, and then he realized she was probably too distraught to climb the bank without help, and he lifted her in his arms to lay her down on the soft grass. She was still sobbing as he pulled his boots on over wet breeches and then knelt to wrap his jacket around her.

"Come, m'lady," he said in his commanding way. "There is nothing to cry about now."

He picked her up in his arms again, a little surprised at how light she was. One slim arm crept up around his neck, and he wondered at the constricted feeling in his throat as she laid her dark head on his chest.

It was nothing more than relief, of course, he told himself, even as he realized it was something a great deal more. As he strode toward the hall, he heard her whisper, "I'm—I'm sorry, Father." And then she hiccupped.

William Fairhaven stopped for a moment, to look down into her wet, tear-streaked face. He could not seem to find the searing words of condemnation that had always come so readily to mind before this.

"We will discuss this later, Anne," he said. "Right

now, we both need a hot drink, a large towel, and some dry clothes.''

She hiccupped again and then she closed her eyes. For a moment, the duke thought there was a little smile on her lips, but it was gone quickly. He shook his head, sure he had been mistaken, and continued his march up to the hall.

After a solitary lunch, the duke had more than recovered his usual sangfroid. The lecture he read the twins was delivered in his customary cutting manner. He told them he was most displeased with both their deception and their disobedience. He promised them even further restrictions on their freedom as a result of their willfullness, and he concluded by telling them they were enough to drive a perfectly normal man right out of his mind.

"We beg your pardon, Father," Amelia whispered, twisting the skirt of her gown in both hands and crushing the fabric. The duke, who was about to point out how unbecoming this was, held his tongue when he saw the tears in her eyes.

"I must thank you for saving me, Father," Lady Anne volunteered, identical tears filling her eyes. "I will never, ever, go fishing again."

"Try not to be so dramatic, Anne," the duke said coldly. "Of course you will go fishing again. But you will not go out in a boat unless you are accompanied by someone who can swim."

At the girls' eager nod of agreement, he added, "*Any* kind of boat up to and including a ship of the line, on *any* body of water, no matter how small or shallow, *any*where in the world. I trust I have covered every eventuality?"

They nodded again, and he dismissed them, setting them the task of writing a four-page essay each on filial disobedience as a punishment.

"And to think I lost the fish, too," Lady Anne mourned as if she considered that quite enough punishment in itself. "And it must have weighed over four pounds!"

The duke resisted calling her a number of names that came readily to his mind now and contented himself by pointing sternly to the door.

After the twins had curtsied and gone off to do his bidding, he ran a hand over his smooth dark hair and sighed. He realized that never had he regretted his wife's untimely death more.

He stood brooding beside his desk for a moment, and then he sat down and dipped a quill in the silver inkwell. He would ask the Lady Juliet to advise him. He might not agree with everything she said about the correct way to raise young ladies, but he had to have some kind of assistance before one or both of the twins managed to kill themselves. And even if all they succeeded in doing was to drive him to distraction, that was quite bad enough, he told himself, his lips compressed.

Juliet was surprised and not overly pleased when his note arrived at the manse. In it, he begged her to let him take her for a drive that same afternoon, saying only that he needed her advice.

Juliet did not like the arrogant duke, but although she wished she might refuse, she penned an acceptance and gave it to the waiting groom. As she changed her gown, she wondered what Anne and Amelia had been up to now.

An hour later, as the duke helped her to the perch of his phaeton, he complimented her on her amber driving dress and dashing feather-trimmed bonnet. Lady Juliet thanked him formally, without smiling, and he wondered at it as he took up the reins and nodded to his tiger to let 'em go.

The slight young man in the duke's livery swung up

behind with the expertise that came from long experience.

There was no conversation until the busy village street had been negotiated, but when the open road was reached and the duke dropped his hands and the team settled into a fast trot, he said, "No doubt you are wondering why I asked to see you, m'lady?"

"As if I have to wonder about that," she said, smiling a little at last. "Tell me, what have they done now?"

The duke's face was cold as he told her about the twins' deception and the way Anne had almost drowned.

Wisely, Juliet did not point out that since Anne had been able to reach the punt and hang on, she had been in no danger whatsoever. At thirteen, she was as agile as a boy, and Juliet knew she could have kicked her way to shore pushing the punt before her. She wondered why Anne had not mentioned this to the duke, although for her sake she was glad the girl had concealed it. If the duke were to realize he had made such a heroic rescue unnecessarily, it would do nothing for his self-esteem. In fact, Juliet mused, he would probably be furious. He was not at all the kind of man who would see the amusing side of it, and he would hate being the butt of any joke. He was, after all, the Duke of Severn.

"I am about at my wit's end, ma'am," he was saying now. "It does not seem to matter how I forbid them to do these things, they only manage to find something else I have not thought to prohibit to get themselves in trouble. I never realized young girls could be so—so trying!"

His voice was so acerbic that Lady Juliet had no trouble stifling the laughter she could feel rising in her throat.

"Although, as I have often remarked," he went on at his most urbane again, "women of any age seem to delight in being difficult. No doubt they feel it makes them more interesting."

Before Juliet could object to his sweeping condemnation of her sex, he turned to her and said, "But come, ma'am. Give me the benefit of your advice. You were thirteen once, although I doubt very much that the cool elegant lady that you have become was ever such a hoyden as my daughters at that age."

Juliet looked down at the hands she had clasped in her lap, neat in York tan gloves. She was only too aware of the duke's proximity, that broad shoulder touching hers and his warm breath so close she could feel it stirring in her hair. And the light in those dark eyes when he paid her that polished compliment, the devilish slant of those heavy eyebrows, the rueful little smile on his mouth, were things she did not care to contemplate for too long. He made her supremely uneasy—no, more than that, he frightened her. She had vowed that no man would ever do so again, and remembering this vow, she took a deep breath to steady herself before she said, "As we discussed the other day, your Grace, I am hardly the expert. However, if it were up to me, I would not try to remedy the omissions of thirteen years in such a short time."

"I have never been known to be lacking in understanding, but I am afraid I do not follow you," the duke said, looking straight ahead now as he gave a farmer's cart loaded with hay the go-by.

"The twins have gone their merry way for a number of years, and they have been little checked," Juliet explained. "Now, suddenly, their father swoops down on them and seems determined to change them into patterns of propriety in the twinkling of an eye. Being as spirited as they are, they object most strenuously to his program. You must remember they are only thirteen and used to joining in all their brothers' adventures. It is much too soon to expect them to be interested in society and manners and presenting a ladylike appearance."

She glanced sideways to see the duke glaring at her. "But as the Duke of Severn, I must insist on it, madam," he said, his voice cold.

Juliet swallowed a quick retort and tried to say gently, "It is unfortunate that their mother did not live so they could have learned their manners at her knee and taken their cue from her as to what constitutes the correct behavior for a gently bred female. Instead, there were only their brothers and the servants as role models. They will change, your Grace, but not until they are a little older."

The duke seemed to hear some condemnation in her voice for his absence all those years, and he said stiffly, "Was that the way your mother saw to your upbringing, Lady Juliet?"

To his surprise, she did not answer at once, and when he glanced down at her, he saw that she was frowning, "Oh, my mother was the epitome of femininity," she said at last. "She was all sensibility, full of romantic whims, and had such a tender heart and was so frightened by the world that she had to be constantly supported by her loved ones lest she sink into a depression of the spirits that would quite overset her."

The duke was delighted he had never had to deal with the late Lady Manchester, but he wondered at the dry little tone her daughter had used to describe her. "If you have drawn her correctly, it is obvious that you did not pattern yourself after her. I do not think you a woman given to fits of sensibility or depression, and somehow I cannot picture you indulging in romantic whims," he said, his voice wry. When the Lady Juliet did not answer and allowed him to see only her cameo profile, he added, "But if what you say is true, I am astonished she was brave enough to travel to America."

"She felt it was the only course open to her," Juliet said at last. "My father left her in comfortable circumstances, but not a woman of great wealth, and as you know, my brother is not interested in worldly matters. My mother did not want to live in some backwater, and so she was forced to emigrate. In Louisiana she was pampered and petted and she could enjoy the luxury she craved."

She stopped suddenly, her face paler now, and then she said in a different tone, "But you hardly took me driving to discuss my mother, your Grace. Come, may I speak frankly to you about the twins?"

The duke nodded, "I would appreciate it, ma'am."

Juliet thought he sounded stiff, as if he rarely had to ask anyone for help and had discovered he did not care for the role of petitioner.

"I think you would find it easier if you proceeded more slowly, sir," she said. "Do not set the twins to such long study hours. Let them amuse themselves part of the time as they were wont to do. And do not always criticize and correct them. Show them you care for them and love them."

The duke's black eyebrows soared. "But of course I care for them. Otherwise, I would not put myself to the trouble of remaining here all this time," he told her, his voice stiff.

"But they do not know that. They feel you are demanding these unreasonable things only because their behavior reflects on you, not because you love them and wish to help them," Lady Juliet replied.

The duke snorted, and she was quick to add, "There can be a special bond between girls and their father, your Grace. It is different from any relationship he might have with his sons. Most girls adore their fathers, indeed, idealize them."

The duke's laugh was harsh with disbelief. "I can

66

assure you, dear lady, that neither Anne nor Amelia idealizes or adores me.''

"Not at the moment," she agreed, her voice calm. "But in time they will come to do so, and then you will never again be the Dreadful Duke.''

"The *what*?'' he snapped, dropping his hands so the team broke into a canter.

Juliet wished with all her heart that she had not let slip that particular nickname the twins used so often. "I do beg your pardon, sir," she said. "You are with them so seldom, and never in very happy circumstances, so that is what they have come to consider you. But in time you will be their—their wonderful father, I am sure.''

Suddenly reminded of the tiger perched behind her, Juliet stopped speaking and stiffened. The duke shook his head. "I would not wager a ha'penny on it if I were you, m'lady," he said. Then he caught sight of her backward glance and he added, "Do not fear to say whatever you like. My tiger is deaf and dumb and he cannot write. I chose him for those attributes especially, and I have never been more glad of it than today. The Dreadful Duke, indeed!''

Lady Juliet thought he was living up to his nickname more every time she met him. Imagine choosing a servant for his abnormalities. The duke *was* a dreadful man, but she was not in the least surprised. In her experience, there were few men who could not be designated that way.

Back at Severn Hall, the twins were working diligently on their essays, both dark heads bent over their desks. For a while there was nothing but the sound of their scratching quills in the comfortable, cluttered schoolroom that had known so many generations of Fairhaven children. On one corner of Anne's desk there was a crude carving of the initials W.F., followed by the date 1780.

"How do you spell *filial*?" Anne asked, screwing up her face in concentration and little knowing she was sitting in her father's place.

Amelia flipped back a page and read, "F-e-e-l-e-a-l. It doesn't look right somehow, does it?"

Anne wrote it down, the tip of her pink tongue protruding from the corner of her mouth. Then she sighed and put her pen down to rub her ink-stained fingers. "This is very hard, Melia, especially since I can't write about how there was no need to save me at all. I had to pretend to be drowning when I saw his face. Why, he looked almost frightened, as if he really did care for me."

She frowned, and then she picked up her essay and complained, "I have only filled two pages and I have said every single thing I could think of on the subject."

"I've said some things twice," Lady Amelia admitted, leaning over to read her twin's essay. "I hope mentioning the fish that got away again will not put him in a towering rage," she said. "Or going on and on about how nice it was on the lake this morning."

"I couldn't think of anything else," Anne told her.

"But what does fishing have to do with obedience?" Amelia asked.

Her twin shrugged. "It fills the page," she answered, and then she asked, "I wonder what they are doing now?"

Amelia had no trouble following the abrupt change of subject. "Talking about us, of course," she said.

"That's not very romantic," Anne complained.

"You can't be romantic in an open phaeton, tooling along the post road with a tiger up behind, not even when the tiger's Henry," Amelia told her, and then she grinned. "Especially when every Tom, Dick, and Harry might come along and see you."

Her twin giggled, her eyes sparkling. "Perhaps they will stop somewhere and leave Henry to watch the team," she said. "Perhaps they will take a walk to be alone, and then the duke will hug and kiss her."

"I don't think he'll do that," Amelia protested. "He hardly knows her, and besides, he is not given much to hugs and kisses. He's never given *us* any."

"He hugged me this morning," Anne said brightly, and then her face grew gloomy. "I don't think Juliet would like it if he did," she said.

"No, I wouldn't like a strange man to do it either," Amelia agreed. "Anne, do you think we are doing the right thing trying to get Juliet to fall in love with the Dreadful Duke? I know it would take Father's mind from us if they got married, but is it really fair to our friend to condemn her to such an awful life just so we can be more comfortable?"

Anne appeared to consider this seriously. "But ladies seem to like getting married, although I can't imagine why," she said at last. "And even if Father is stern and cold and sarcastic now, you know when he is married he might change. Look at Bob Randall, the groom. He's all smiles and jokes since he married Lucy, and before he was an awful bear."

"I suppose," Amelia said slowly. "Do you think Father likes Juliet, twin?" she asked.

"He laughed several times last night, and he even smiled at her. Seven times. I was counting," Anne replied. "And you know he has never smiled from the day he arrived until she came to dinner."

Amelia nodded, remembering her father's customary expression. "We will have to think of ways so they keep meeting each other, Anne," she said. "We can't expect Father to ask her to dinner all the time."

"Well, he did take her driving today," Anne said.

"But only because we did wrong this morning," her twin was quick to point out.

There was a sudden, abrupt silence in the school-room, broken only by the ticking of the old wall clock. Both girls stared at each other, and then Amelia put both hands to her mouth and shook her head, almost as if she were frightened. Anne held her eye until she was forced to nod reluctantly at last.

"It's the only way, Melia," she said gruffly. "I dare-say we won't have to write too many of these ghastly essays, and he won't beat us too hard or too often."

"But he never beats us," Amelia whispered.

"I don't think we can count on that anymore," Anne said, determined to be honest. "We shall just have to remember that it's for a good cause, and be brave."

Amelia gulped and nodded again, and then both girls put their heads together to plan the next move of their campaign, a pair of most unlikely cupids.

6

By the time the Duke of Severn returned Lady Juliet to the manse, he had agreed to several things, perhaps more stung by his daughter's nickname for him than he cared to admit. The twins were only to spend a few hours each day at their desks, alhtough he said he would amend this schedule if he felt the additional freedom was leading them into trouble again. He also promised to propose some amusements they might enjoy in his company, and the Lady Juliet was once again begged to visit the hall on a regular basis. The twins would have cheered if they could have known of this particular concession.

Juliet thanked him for the drive when he lifted her down at the front gate of the manse. Her voice and demeanor were cool and contained, but the duke noticed how quickly she stepped away from him, almost before he had released her waist as her sandals touched the ground. He looked at her coldly, for he was not at all used to this kind of reaction from the ladies he so honored. Was it possible that she did not care for him, perhaps even found him repulsive? he wondered as he climbed to his seat again after escorting her to the door. Had he imagined that her arm had trembled when he first cupped her elbow to help her up the flagged walk? He was frowning as he drove the team between the gates of Severn, not even seeing his gatekeeper's bow or the way the man's wife and children had lined up to give him obeisance.

It could not be physical distaste, he told himself as the phaeton rumbled over the arched bridge halfway up the drive. He knew he was a handsome man, his figure trim and well-muscled and without an ounce of fat. His dress, although conservative, was always in the first stare of fashion, and he was a fastidious man as well. He bathed every day, wore fresh linen, and was particular about his teeth and breath. What could it be? Perhaps she had a dislike for tall, dark men in general? Or perhaps she fancied herself in love with someone else, he pondered, tossing the reins to his tiger as they reached the stableyard.

He did not return to the hall at once, but began to walk through the park. That must be it! He had been told too many times of his masculine magnetism to believe it otherwise, and he knew, from their easy capitulation, his power over the fair sex. Perhaps the Lady Juliet feared he might undermine her faithfulness to her lover.

The duke stared down at the patterns of light and shade under the massive elms as he walked along, his hands clasped behind his back. But if the lady was in love with another man, why had she buried herself down here in Devon, and by her own admission had no interest in London society? If the man she loved was in America, why had she put the width of the ocean between them? And why had she never married?

He removed his beaver and ran a hand over his hair. It did not make sense. He decided to watch her carefully in the days ahead and question her more particularly. There had been something in her voice when she spoke of her mother, and something of relief when she changed the subject. The little mystery that was the Lady Juliet Manchester would be a welcome puzzle for him to solve while he was a prisoner here in the country, and it would relieve his boredom.

It was not, of course, he told himself, that he cared a snap of his fingers for the woman, but his pride was bruised to think that she did not find him attractive. Perhaps he would go further. Perhaps he would bend all his considerable charm to making her fall in love with him, as a way of amusing himself. Anne and Amelia, for all they were his major concern and took up so much of his time, could not fill every hour of the day—or the night.

He stopped and smiled to himself. Perhaps the lady might even be cajoled beyond a light flirtation into an affair. She was no child. She had told him she was thirty-one, and she would know the rules as well as he did himself. And if he discovered she was not prepared to amuse herself that way, he would settle for dalliance, a light sparring with words, a few stolen kisses.

Feeling better, he turned and made his way back to the hall. Up in the third-floor schoolroom, his daughters retreated from the window and scurried back to their desks. They had taken it as a very good sign that he had gone off by himself right after leaving Juliet, but they had no time to discuss this, for they still had another page each to write on "feeleal" disobedience before tea.

Two days later, by prior arrangement, Lady Juliet came up to the hall. The twins were delighted to see her, and since it was a bright, early September day, the three set off on a long ramble, accompanied by two of the dogs. Of the duke there was no sign, and for that Juliet could only be grateful. She seemed a little abstracted as the girls chattered, a fact they noticed almost at once and commented on by exchanging a pregnant glance.

"Father has driven to Barnstaple this afternoon on business, Juliet," Anne told her casually.

"He said he was very sorry to miss your visit, very sorry indeed," Amelia confided, most untruthfully.

"But he mentioned a jaunt to the coast if the weather continues fine," Anne went on.

"Do say you will come with us, Juliet," Amelia begged. "It will make up for the trip we planned that Father would not allow us to take earlier."

Juliet agreed, a little absently, and then she asked how they were getting along now.

"It is the most amazing thing," Anne said, skipping a little in her delight. "Father has been almost pleasant."

"Why, he even smiled when he read our essays," her twin said. "And it did not take us *too* long to correct the spelling, did it, Anne?"

"Perhaps we should make sure he has a dip in the lake more often." Anne laughed. "It has made him almost human."

"I do hope you have stopped baiting him, you bad girls," Juliet scolded them lightly. "I could not believe my eyes the night I came to dinner. You were deliberately provoking, doing things that you outgrew years ago. Your bad table manners, scowls, and reticence were enough to make anyone cross."

Amelia spoke up, "Well, we are trying, but—"

"—do not be surprised if we slip a little, dear Juliet," Anne said, finishing the sentence.

Lady Juliet stopped and took both their hands.

"Now, what are you planning? Come now, tell me at once!"

"Nothing at all," both twins said earnestly in unison.

"Oh, see, isn't that a fox over there?" Anne asked, pointing to a distant thicket.

"Where?" Amelia asked, and the dangerous subject of their future behavior was successfully bypassed.

The duke came back while they were having tea in one of the smaller salons. Anne jumped up and begged him to join them, and he bowed to Lady Juliet and looked a question, as if to ask her permission to do so.

"If you would care for it, your Grace," she said, eyes lowered as she readied another cup.

"Very much, thank you," he said, his voice warm, as he took the seat beside her and gave her an intimate smile. Silently, Anne warned Amelia not to show any delight over this promising development.

Anne passed her father the plate of cakes. He took it from her quickly, remembering an earlier teatime when she had spilled it all over his buckskin breeches. His valet had had a devil of a time with the whipped-cream and raspberry-jam stains.

"How far did you progress this morning, m'ladies?" he asked his daughters as Lady Juliet poured his tea.

"We have reached the Hundred Years War," Amelia said, sounding as if she felt it had taken them a hundred years to do so.

"And the Black Death . . . ugh!" Anne said with a bright smile quite at odds with her gruesome subject.

The duke watched her bite into another eclair with gusto, and restrained a shudder. "Well, that is one way to describe pestilence, I suppose," he said. "It was a very unfortunate period of history, and many people died. Perhaps that would be a better way to characterize it?"

"It is really important to know all these things, Father?" Amelia asked, for she was not at all a scholar.

"After all, the thirteen-hundreds were all so long ago." Her sign spoke volumes.

"As daughters of the Duke of Severn, of course it is important. You are of the ruling class, and it is your duty to know your country's history. If you do not, who will?" the duke asked sternly.

"Sometimes I wonder if being a little scullery maid would not be better, after all," Anne remarked, made brave by Juliet's presence and her father's more relaxed attitude.

"Much better," Amelia agreed.

The frown that this artless confession brought to the duke's face told the twins immediately of their error.

"You are mistaken, m'ladies," he said coldly. "There is nothing admirable about being an ignorant maid. You would be overworked, ill-fed, and perhaps abused. Certainly your hands would be in a constant state of rough, painful redness, and you would have nothing to look forward to but hard work until you died. You should thank God you were born to the nobility, to the benefits of an education, and to privilege. It is your duty to be worthy of these privileges and to take advantage of the opportunities that are yours by birth. Do not let me hear either of you make such a ridiculous statement again. Remember, you are Fairhavens of Severn."

Both girls looked down into their teacups and murmured an assent, and Lady Juliet took the first breath she had drawn since the beginning of the duke's lecture.

"I can assure you you would not care for it, m'ladies," she said, smiling a little at them and trying to lighten the atmosphere. "Maids have even less freedom than you do, and only a few hours off each month. It is a very confining life; your father is correct."

She rose before the girls could answer, and the duke set his teacup down and rose as well.

"You must excuse me, m'ladies, your Grace," she

said, picking up her reticule and gloves. "My brother will be wondering where I am."

"Are you—are you going to take the Lady Juliet home, Father?" Amelia asked, her blue eyes wide with innocence.

"That is not at all necessary, your Grace," Juliet said quickly. "I would not put you to the trouble and I would prefer to be alone."

The duke bowed, his dark face enigmatic, as she curtsied in farewell. He was so ataken back at the abrupt way he had been dismissed that he did not go with her to the door, and when the twins would have done so, he motioned them to their seats again. "The Lady Juliet can find her own way out, I am sure," he said, his hooded eyes bleak. "There are still some questions I wish to ask you."

Anne sighed and settled back in her chair, but Amelia called after Juliet, "Do not forget, m'lady! We will send you word as soon as the day is decided for our trip to the coast."

Lady Juliet smiled a little and slipped out the door. The duke had not been aware that she was to be included in the treat, and after the way he had just been dismissed, he was a little annoyed. But then he realized that it could only advance his plans for the lady, and feeling challenged by her continued coldness to him, he began to look foward to it.

Unfortunately, a storm confined everyone indoors for the next three days. Two days later, the twins sent an excited message to the manse announcing that they were to leave at ten the following morning. Lady Juliet wrote a civil but firm refusal.

Anne and Amelia were disappointed. "How could she contract a sore throat now, when she knew we were going to the seashore?" Anne asked her sister crossly.

As was their custom just before they went to sleep,

both girls were curled up in Amelia's four-poster, discussing this setback.

Amelia shook her head. "It does seen contrary of her, doesn't it?" she asked. "But you know, Anne, I do not think she looked at all pleased when we first proposed the scheme. And then to refuse Father's escort home after tea the other day . . . well! I think Juliet is being difficult beyond words."

Her sister nodded, deep in thought. "It made him angry, too," she said. And then she bounced a little on the thick mattress and said, "Remember the parties he sometimes brought to Severn, twin? There was always one beautiful lady who seemed to think Father was just *wonderful!* I think he is cross because Juliet acts as if he were nothing out of the common way."

"To think of it! How *dare* she, when he is William Fairhaven, the Duke of Severn?" Amelia said, her words solemn and measured.

Both girls collapsed in laughter, hugging each other in delight, and for the moment, their promotion of the duke's and Juliet's future alliance was forgotten. It would have been too much to say that either one of them forgot it, however.

The duke and his daughters stopped to deliver a bouquet of flowers to Lady Juliet the next day before they set out on their drive. Reverend Manchester was the only one about to receive them, for Juliet had retired to her room. Her throat was not at all sore, but she did not feel she could listen to Romeo bemoan her loss of such a pleasant time once more. She had determined, therefore, to spend the day by herself, reading and writing letters.

As the open landau from Severn pulled away from the manse, she could not help staring out her bedchamber window at the duke, and she felt a cold shiver run over her body as she did so. It had been a long time since any man had been able to make her feel anything but distaste, but whenever the duke was near, her knees shook, her skin grew hot and cold by turns, and she began to quiver. It was all very well to tell herself she was being ridiculous, but no matter how she chastised herself and promised to keep a firm control over her emotions, he had only to turn those dark eyes and mocking smile her way for her breath to catch in her throat and her heart to begin to pound alarmingly in her breast.

She had refused the expedition for just these reasons. Much as she liked the twins, she knew she must curtail their friendship until their father left Severn again. The emotions that dueled in her breast were so strong they made her feel ill: on the one hand, there was the revulsion she always felt when forced into close contact with any male, and on the other, an irresistible longing to move closer still to this particular one.

She felt as if she might be losing her mind. How was it possible to be attracted to the very thing that you knew only too well would hurt you? It was behavior as incomprehensible as that of any moth beating itself to death against a lamp.

Then there were the infantile daydreams she was suffering. She, waltzing at a grand ball with the duke, or strolling some moonlit garden held tight in his strong arm while he murmured love words to her. She, melting into his arms, her own going up around his neck to pull that strong, handsome face down to hers, while he held her so close to him she felt as if they were one flesh indeed. These were the childish dreams of a young girl's first infatuation, and she was thirty-one, a woman grown, a woman more aware than most that any involvement with the opposite sex could only lead to pain and tragedy.

The duke was a proud, arrogant, conceited, uncaring, cold, self-serving, hurtful, selfish, treacherous, perfidious, punishing *man*. She must remember that. She must not let down her guard, not even for an instant. She had vowed she would never allow a man into her life ever again, and she had repeated that vow many times.

She was Juliet Manchester, and she intended to remain Juliet Manchester until she died. She would be strong and resolute; she would not falter or weaken because one of *them* gave her a devilish, sideways glance full of the mischief that men were so intent on. She must not begin to think that the duke was any different from others of his kind. In fact, she suspected he was a great deal worse than many, if the whole truth were to be known. How many women had he loved and left, used and then discarded? She went back to her desk and her letters with renewed determination that she would never be one of them.

In her new militant mood, it was easy for Juliet to refuse the dinner invitation that she and the vicar received a few days later. Since she had made a quick recovery of her sore throat, she was forced to say she had a headache. Juliet did not use this ploy too often, but since her brother, in common with the rest of his sex, seemed to equate headaches with the female condition, he did not press her on this occcasion, but went off to Severn by himself.

And then, early in the morning two days later, Juliet was startled to discover that the duke had called at the manse and was demanding to see her.

"Oh, yes, indeed, milady," Phyllis told her, her eyes wide. "He says he won't go away until you come down, for it's a matter of life and death!"

"Life and death, Phyllis?" Juliet asked, looking skeptical. "Are you sure he said that?"

The maid lowered her eyes, looking mulish. "Well, he looks like it is anyway," she muttered.

Juliet laughed and told her to say she would be with her caller presently.

79

When she slipped into the parlor, she found him striding up and down the small room, looking very much out of place. He appeared so very tall beneath the low ceiling that he seemed to loom over her, but the first *frisson* she felt was quickly gone when she saw his worried face.

"Your Grace," she said as she curtsied.

Before she could ask how she could help him, the duke said harshly, "They are gone. Both of them. Would you have any idea where, ma'am?"

"I?" she asked. "But you know I have not seen them lately." And then she added tartly, "For heaven's sake, sit down! You are enough to make a saint nervous with that frantic pacing."

Surprised, the duke took the nearest chair.

"When did you discover them missing?" Juliet asked, taking the seat across from him. Her voice was calm and even, for she was sure the twins were playing yet another trick on their father.

"They were not in their beds when the housemaid went up to wake them this morning," the duke told her. "It did not look as if they had slept there at all. I have men out searching the park and the woods, while I myself came immediately to see whether they have come here."

Juliet shook her head, a little perturbed now. All the unpleasant sensations of being so close to him were gone now as she considered the problem. Although she knew Anne and Amelia often slipped out of the hall after dark, to her knowledge they had never stayed out all night before. Where could they be?

"Do you know of any special activity in the neighborhood, sir?" she asked. "Perhaps a country fair, a barn raising, or even a harvest fete?"

The duke frowned, deep in thought, and then he had to admit he did not.

"Have the twins been talking about one particular subject more than usual?" Juliet persisted.

On reflection, the duke had to shake his head again. The only subject the twins constantly referred to, or so it seemed to him, was the Lady Juliet Manchester.

"Perhaps the servants have been talking of something out of the ordinary?" the lady asked next.

The duke's eyes grew keen and he sat up straighter, his face growing even colder and sterner. "The other day my head groom did say that there had been signs of gypsies in the vicinity of Eggesford," he said through lips that seemed to have turned to stone. "But surely the twins could not have heard anything about that."

"Oh, your Grace," Juliet admonished him with a shake of her head. "Of course they did! There is nothing to equal the flow of gossip in any house, be it large or small. If our cook hears a tidbit in the village, you may be sure it comes to my ear not an hour later. And Severn, even as huge and rambling as it is, is no different, except that there are more people about to spread the news."

"But—but Eggesford is several miles away, and the twins would never be so rash as to go there, and at night too, to see a company of Egyptians. You forget I have told them over and over what they owe their name, and . . ."

The duke's voice trailed away as his common sense reasserted itself and reminded him that that is exactly where they would go, as fast as their legs could carry them. And then he had a sudden vision of the two of them sitting on the back of a gypsy's cart, swinging their legs above the dust of the road, and laughing together at the adventure that was in store for them.

He rose. "I must get the carriage. You will have time to prepare in the meantime, and then we will set off for Eggesford at once."

"We?" Lady Juliet asked, looking affronted.

"This is no time for missishness, m'lady," he snapped as he picked up his gloves and his crop. "I need you and I have no time to beg you most humbly to assist me. I depend on you. Fifteen minutes, no more."

The door slammed behind him, and for a moment Juliet sat stunned. Then she hurried up to change and write a note to her brother. The duke was quite capable of carrying her out and depositing her in his carriage while she was wearing nothing but a morning dress and house slippers, she knew. And truly, she was concerned for the twins, although she tried not to think about them or in what circumstances they might find themselves even now. Gypsies! Some were kind, but some, as she knew, were cruel. And in a few years, Anne and Amelia were going to be such beautiful girls.

She was waiting at the gate when the duke's carriage arrived, and she stepped up to join him without waiting for anyone to help her. She noticed that beside the coachman and the three grooms, there were four outriders as well. The duke was prepared for trouble, but the sight did not reassure her as she took her seat beside him.

She was remembering the time long ago when a strange man had followed her as she walked along a country road alone. It was coming on to dusk and there was no one else in sight as she made her way home from the village to her father's estate. Her mother had never insisted she take a maid, for she was only twelve, and everyone in the area knew the Lady Juliet.

For some reason, this strange man frightened her. When she slowed or quickened her pace, she could hear from the thudding of his boots that he was matching her step for step. At last she had been alarmed enough to break into a run when she saw the gates ahead of her. As she ran up the drive toward safety, she had turned her head to look back. He was standing in the road staring after her and laughing while he pretended to unbutton his breeches. She remembered that after she had told her mother of the incident, she had never been allowed out again without a servant in attendance.

She could still recall how her heart had pounded with a dread of something nameless and unknown that even at twelve she had realized was dark and evil, and she said a fervent prayer that Anne and Amelia might be safe from such horrors. Horrors, that at thirty-one she knew to her sorrow were all too real.

The duke's shoulder brushed hers as the carriage took a curve in the road at speed, but she did not shudder or move away. She was not even aware of him, or the fact that she might be alone with him in a closed carriage for many hours to come.

7

"I shall most certainly beat them when I get my hands on them," the duke said, his words stiff and determined. He startled Juliet considerably, for, lost in her dark memories and her fears for the twins, she had forgotten he was even beside her.

"I have never done so before," he continued, his eyes staring at the bucolic scenery outside the carriage window as if he did not even see it, "but in this instance, I fear Anne and Amelia need to feel my whip about their sides. They have been too much indulged, and now we see the result of it."

Juliet stiffened, remembering that it was she who had convinced the duke to relax the iron grasp that he had used to confine his daughters. She almost cried out in her defense, but then she remembered how distraught he was, and she bit her lip instead.

"They should be punished, certainly, your Grace," she agreed. "Such mad starts are not at all appropriate for the daughters of the Duke of Severn."

The duke's frown deepened, and she wondered at it, for her voice had been mild and conciliatory. "I hope they keep that information between their teeth," he said grimly, as if he were gritting his own.

At his companion's questioning glance, he explained, "If these Egyptians know what prizes they have, it will cost me a king's portion to recover the girls."

"You think they might kidnap them? Hold them for ransom, sir?" Juliet asked, her voice horrified.

"Why wouldn't they?" the duke replied. "Gypsies are not so blessed with worldly goods that they would turn down such a golden opportunity. Besides, as you must be aware, they steal everything they can. Nothing is safe from them. Nothing."

He frowned again, and then he settled back against the squabs. The tension in his face and the taut muscles of his body made relaxing a major effort for him, but in a moment he opened the hard fists he had made. Then he turned a little toward her.

"I must thank you for coming with me, Lady Juliet," he said in the sarcastic drawl that she remembered was his usual manner of speaking.

Juliet waved her hand, but when she would have spoken, he added, "It is especially gratifying since I have had the most lowering feeling that you have been avoiding my company. Now, why should that be, do you suppose?"

Juliet felt herself growing cold as the carriage continued to race through the golden September morning. "I am afraid I do not understand you, your Grace," she said evenly, meeting his glance and holding it. She was proud of her self-control.

"Since we have an hour or so before we reach Eggesford, I shall be delighted to explain, and we shall have plenty of time to discuss it, ma'am," he told her.

Juliet's heart sank. Somehow she had thought they would continue to discuss the twins, a very safe subject. As if he knew what she was thinking, he added, "There is no point in going over and over the possible situations my daughters might have stumbled into. It would only be upsetting for us both. We are going to their aid as fast as we can, and until we find them, there is nothing further we can do.

"No, what I propose is that we discuss this strange antipathy you seem to have for me," he told her, his voice determined.

Juliet did not think he sounded as if he would be fobbed off with some simple excuse, or her continued surprise at his suppositions, and she steeled herself for a battle of wits.

"Is no one allowed to feel any dislike for the Duke of Severn, then, sir?" she asked, trying to keep her voice light and amused. "Yet I do not believe any human being can make another like him, no matter how exalted his rank. Why, even King George cannot command his subjects' love."

The duke nodded, as if acknowledging a hit. "I am not so conceited as you appear to think me, m'lady," he agreed calmly. "I will admit, however, that your dislike for me is a new come-out. No doubt you would be the first to say it could only be most beneficial, although, perhaps, long overdue."

He paused, the light in his dark eyes very noticeable, and his handsome mouth quirked in a little smile. Juliet swallowed and inclined her head an inch in haughty agreement.

William Fairhaven laughed out loud, and bowed to her. "My compliments, ma'am! I left myself wide open, did I not, for such a quiet set-down as I can never remember receiving? But this sparring we engage in will not do. You must have some reason. Come, you can tell me. There is not even my deaf-and-dumb tiger in attendance to deter you. Perhaps you dislike dark men in general? Perhaps dukes as a class make you feel ill? Perhaps it is my manner, my conversation, my style of life that offend you? Do feel free to tell me, my dear. I am not likely to become angry at someone who is helping me recover my daughters, after all.''

All the time he had been speaking, Juliet had been searching desperately for some weapon she could use. Now she made herself turn and face him squarely.

"You have forgotten that I was ill the day you took the twins to the coast, your Grace, and that I had the headache the evening of your dinner party. You have imagined a slight I never intended.''

She looked at him for only a moment, and then his dark eyes, which seemed to be searching deep into her heart and mind, made her lower her own eyes to her lap.

"Perhaps you should consult a doctor, m'lady?'' he asked politely. "These continued ailments that you suffer are most distressing.''

When Juliet refused to speak or meet his eyes again, he murmured, "Besides, that was paltry, m'dear. I am sure you can do much better than that.''

"You are impossible, your Grace,'' Juliet blurted out, stung into honesty at last. "You know I am as good as your prisoner here, and as such, at your conversational mercy. I would prefer to discuss any other subject on earth, but of course you will not allow that! It would serve you right if I refused to speak to you at all.''

Those slashing black brows rose even higher. "You would not be so cruel, ma'am,'' he told her evenly. "That would be to condemn us both to our thoughts and imaginings. By the time we reached the gypsy encampment, I, at least, would be ready to do murder.

Spare me that. I have no desire to hang high at Tyburn, drawn and quartered.''

''I am sure you would find some way to escape such punishment, your Grace,'' Juliet told him, her hazel eyes wary. ''What are some nameless Egyptians compared to a duke of the realm, when all is said and done?''

''You are turning the subject, m'lady,'' the duke drawled, and then he reached out and took her hand in his. Juliet gasped and tried to pull it away, her breath coming quickly in her distress.

The duke noticed how her face had paled, throwing the little mole into sharp contrast, and the violent way she began to tremble. He let her go at once, although the stern question in his eark eyes demanded an explanation for her unusual reaction to the simple clasp of two gloved hands.

Her hazel eyes begged him not to question her, but he continued to stare down into her face, waiting. She did not think he seemed angry; in fact, she was surprised at the kindness in his glance.

''I do not like men,'' she said at last, her tight voice little more than a whisper.

''Ah, but what a relief,'' the duke replied easily.

Juliet looked at him suspiciously, almost as if she felt he was mocking her.

''I cannot tell you how you have revived my flagging spirits, dear lady,'' he went on. ''I thought it was only myself you did not like. But if you include half the world's population in your condemnation, I do not have to fear any special failing of my own. You see, I had begun to think there was something distasteful about my person. Now that I know I am only one of the millions you dislike, I can be easy.'' He nodded in satisfaction, and then he asked swiftly, ''Why?''

''Why?'' she repeated, wishing she could look away from that dark, mesmerizing gaze.

"Why don't you like men?" he persisted, almost, she thought wildly, in the same tone of voice he would have employed to inquire why she did not care for mutton or fish.

She lost her temper over his persistence, and she said quickly, "That, your Grace, with all due respect for your exalted station, is none of your concern!"

To her surprise, he laughed. "But you are wrong, Lady Juliet. I have made up my mind that you are to be very much my concern," he told her in his mocking drawl. "I have decided that there is something between us even now, something that should be tended and carefully nourished so it might grow into the consuming, wondrous thing it could be. I have promised myself to bend all my efforts to attain it, and your capitulation as well. How sad it is, that like Romeo in the play, I find my lady so cold, and that like him, 'I am out of favor, where I am in love.' "

Juliet sat very still in her corner of the carriage, trying not to cringe farther away from him. I will not listen to him, she told herself wildly. He is mad. He *must* be mad!

"How dare you treat me to this ranting?" she asked, in her distress forgetting again the cool, composed role she had meant to play. "Here I have come with you to help you find your daughters, and nothing more, and instead I am treated to a madman's discourse on love. I must ask you to put me down at once!"

The duke looked idly past her to where fields and hedgerows stretched to the horizon. "Here?" he asked, waving his hand to the lonely countryside. "I could never in good conscience do so, my dear ma'am. Then I would have three ladies to worry about, and I can assure you, two are quite enough. 'Sufficient unto the day is the evil thereof.' That is not from *Romeo and Juliet,* m'lady. That is from the Bible."

"I am well aware of the source," she told him. "And

I could wish you had spent more of your time reading the Bible, sir, and less on Shakespeare's plays.''

''You must instruct me in it sometime, my dear,'' he told her, tipping his beaver over his eyes and settling back on the squabs once again. His booted legs came up to rest on the opposite seat and he folded his arms over his chest. ''However, since you do not care to converse with me on the subject, I shall go to sleep. No doubt I will need all my wits about me when we arrive at Eggesford. May I suggest you rest as well?''

Juliet stared out the window, grasping the strap beside her as the carriage swayed over some ruts. Softly, from behind her, she heard the duke add, ''We will continue our discussion at some future time. I am interested—most interested, indeed—as to why you have this antipathy for men, and I am determined to discover the reason for it.''

Juliet had no answer, and he fell silent. She was still profoundly shocked by the duke's sudden attack. He had never shown her any signs of the lover before; she had not thought of him as a pursuer. Was his inexplicable behavior the result of her shunning his company? Was he so vain he could not bear to think there might be even one woman in England who would not fall willingly into his arms, and it was only her reluctance to do so that had made him decide on this course?

She stared at the countryside racing by, her mind and spirits unsettled. He had said he intended to find out why she did not like men; she was sure he would not rest until he did so. What could she tell him? she wondered. The truth, of course, was not possible. She had told no one since she had left Louisiana, not even her brother, who, by the nature of his calling, to say nothing of his love for her, would at least try to understand. But if she could not even tell Romeo, surely under no circumstances could she tell the duke. But he could not force her to reveal her past, she told herself. She had only to remain firm in her denials until he grew bored with the game, or left Devon, or found some other woman to intrigue him.

They reached Eggesford by eleven in the morning, and William Fairhaven awoke as the coach slowed on the outskirts of town. By the time the coachman had turned into the yard of the Blue Boar Inn, he was grim-faced and alert, with all signs of his earlier, teasing behavior gone. Without a word to her, he jumped down and strode to where the innkeeper was waiting, a welcoming smile on his broad face. Juliet could not take her eyes from the duke. Under the brim of his hat, his face was stern and cold, and not a trace of an answering smile creased his lips. From the set of his shoulders and his taut, straight back, Juliet knew with what intensity he asked his questions. At last he nodded and spoke a few words before he came back to the carriage. One of the grooms opened the door, and Juliet leaned forward, nothing but concern for the twins in her eyes now. The upsetting interlude they had shared might never have happened.

"The innkeeper tells me a band of gypsies left the vicinity this morning, traveling south," the duke told her. "They were camped in a wood some three miles from here. I propose to go after them at once. They move slowly, so we should catch them up with ease. That is, we will if you do not feel the need for rest and refreshment first, ma'am."

His drawl was cool and polite, but Juliet knew how anxious he was to be on the road again. "Oh, no, let us go on at once," she said, and he gave her a quick, flashing smile before he turned and spoke to the out-riders.

When he had climbed into the carriage again and given the coachman the order to start, she asked, "What will we do if the twins are not in the gypsies' company, your Grace? We do not have proof that they came here in search of the band, after all."

The duke smiled down at her. "But we do have proof, ma'am. The innkeeper tells me Anne and Amelia were seen last night. He does not know them by name, but surely there cannot be two such identical youngsters roaming the lanes and byroads of Devon."

He paused, and then he added, "No, that would be much too improbable. My daughters must be unique, for to even imagine that there might be other parents as bedeviled as I am goes beyond the realm of anything a fickle fate might devise."

Juliet found herself smiling a little at the sarcastic tone of his voice, and then she was startled as he drew a pistol from the pocket set in the coach door beside him. He began to check it to be sure it was loaded.

"Surely you do not think it will come to that, your Grace," she protested, horrified as she stared at the shining steel of the long barrel and the businesslike trigger.

"We must hope not, m'lady," he agreed, his drawl very noticeable now. "But it is always well to be prepared for any eventuality."

He put the pistol in his coat pocket, and Juliet drew a deep breath.

"I should, of course, prefer to give up a sum of money for my daughters, but if I am denied that, I shall be forced to other measures," he told her. "My men are armed as well. I do not think we will run into much resistance." Then he snorted and added, "Knowing the twins as well as I do now, I would be very much surprised if the gypsy chief did not *beg* me to take them off his hands. It is entirely possible that he will offer to pay me to do so. They have been with him for some hours, more than enough time to get into mischief and upset all his peace and that of the tribe as well."

Before Juliet could answer, she heard voices calling out, and the carriage stopped abruptly. She found herself sliding forward, and was sure she was about to be deposited in a heap on the floorboards, but the duke reached out and put a strong arm across her body to keep her from falling. She had no time to react to this sudden contact, for the arm was withdrawn at once as he turned to the window. Peering around his shoulder, Juliet saw a woebegone little figure standing a short distance away, and she gave a cry of relief.

Even dressed in breeches and boots, with her hair bundled up under a boy's cap, and dirty and exhausted as well, it was obvious that they had found one of the twins.

"Come here at once," the duke ordered, and the slight figure hurried to the carriage to be hauled inside and settled firmly on the facing seat. Now the girl was so close, Juliet could see the fright in her eyes and the tears that had made white channels on her dirty cheeks. She clenched her hands together to keep from exclaiming again.

"Which are you?" the duke demanded brusquely, still holding her arms in a tight grasp.

"Anne, Father," she said. "Oh, I am so glad you have come! But we must make haste, sir, for the gypsies are already on the road and they have taken Melia and—"

"That will be quite enough, Anne," the duke said, his harsh voice so authoritative that she fell silent at once.

"I will do the talking, and you will only answer my questions," he said, his dark eyes never leaving her face. "There is no sense in racing on until we have all the facts. Now, when did the gypsies break camp?"

"Early this morning, Father," Anne whispered, her blue eyes intent on his. She spoke quickly, as if to force him to order the coach into motion again, but the duke continued to speak in his maddening, slow drawl.

"Here, take this handkerchief and wipe your face," he ordered. "You look like a chimney sweep's boy." He handed her a snowy-white square, and Anne did as she was bade.

"How came they to have Amelia, and how did you escape?" he asked next.

"When we found the camp, we decided it would be safer if only one of us talked to them at a time," Anne told them, her eyes going to Juliet as if to seek some reassurance there.

Juliet tried to smile at the girl, but it was a poor effort.

"Melia went in first, because she said if there was any trouble, it would be easier for me to get home and bring you to her aid. I ride better, you see."

"You had a horse?" the duke asked.

"We—we took one from Mr. Harden's field, sir," Anne whispered, lowering her eyes.

"That is the same farmer whose shed you burned on Midsummer's Eve, is it not?" he asked. At her little nod, he murmured, "I do not think Mr. Harden will care to remain at Severn much longer. Perhaps he is making plans to leave even now. But come, where is his horse?"

"The gypsies found where we had tied it in the woods. They—they took it, too."

"Where were you while all this was going on?" the duke asked next.

"Up a tree," Anne told him. "They did not think to look there."

The duke's slashing brows drew together in a frown, and for a long moment his cold eyes ranged over his daughter's clothing; the tight worn breeches and dirty shirt, the scuffed, dusty boots. His expression did not change, but Anne blushed crimson.

"Why did they take Amelia with them?" he continued after a painful silence.

"They plan to sell her, Father. Why, just think of it! Amelia!" Anne exclaimed, leaning forward in distress. She put a hand on his knee and implored, "Please, please, we must go to her at once. We must make haste!"

"Kindly remove that grimy paw from my breeches, daughter," the duke said coldly. Anne drew back as if stung. "We shall go when I say so, and not a moment before."

Juliet bit back an acid comment. It was obvious that Anne was almost hysterical. Why did her father treat her this way? Time enough for cold sarcasm when they were safe back at Severn.

"Do they know she is not the boy she pretends?" he asked next.

"I think so," Anne told him, tears welling up in her eyes. "I followed them back to camp and saw them give Amelia into the care of an old gypsy woman. Why," she added, her voice awed, "she must be almost a hundred years old, she was so bent and wrinkled."

"I do not require a description, Anne. Do try to keep to the point," the duke admonished her.

Anne flushed again. "She took Melia into one of the caravans," she continued in a cracked little voice. "When she came out again alone, she was laughing and saying things I could not understand. But she made some motions . . ."

Her voice died away, and her father ordered, "Describe them!"

Slowly Anne's hands traced an hourglass, and Juliet could not stifle a gasp.

"Very well," the duke said. "I believe we have all the information we need at this time. Excuse me, m'lady. I must speak to the men."

He nodded to Juliet and stepped down from the carriage to stride forward, beckoning the outriders to his side. Juliet reached over and took Anne's cold hands in hers. The girl was crying in earnest now, sobbing and shaking in her distress.

"Come now, Anne," Juliet said, patting her hands. "You are safe, and I am sure Melia will be so as well, in a very short time. Your father will not let anything happen to her."

"I know," Anne wailed. "I did not cry before, not really, but now that he is here, I have turned into a watering pot. Isn't that strange?" She paused for a moment, as if pondering this peculiar behavior, and then she said, "Oh, m'lady, it has just been awful, and we thought it would be such a lark! But since I was the one who thought up the adventure, I should be their captive, not Melia. I am so much braver than she is. I cannot bear to think how frightened she must be without me."

Juliet leaned forward and hugged her, and then she saw the duke approaching. "Your father is coming back. Sit up, Anne, and wipe your eyes. You must compose yourself, for you know your crying will only annoy him."

Anne sniffed and wiped her eyes, nodding a little. By the time the duke took his seat again and had banged on the roof, she had herself under some semblance of control.

Her father eyed her coldly. "When we return to Severn, Anne, we will have time to discuss this debacle in more detail. But right now, there is something I still must know."

Anne stared at him, intrigued but still a little frightened. "Did any of the gypsy men, er, touch Amelia?" he demanded, his voice harsh with worry.

Juliet felt the hair rise on the back of her neck as she waited for the girl's answer, and she was relieved beyond measure when she saw Anne shake her head, her innocent expression confused, as if she wondered at the question.

"Very well," the duke said, sitting back and relaxing at last.

When Juliet saw he was not going to speak again, she asked, "So the gypsies still do not know there are two of you, Anne? They think Melia was alone?"

Anne nodded, and the duke turned toward his companion. "Now, what do you have in your mind, ma'am?" he asked, his dark eyes narrowed.

"It occurred to me that we might make use of that fact, your Grace," she explained. "If they do not know there is a twin, wouldn't it give them pause if Anne stepped down from the carriage when we caught them up? I believe gypsies are very superstitious. It might be that identical twins are considered bad luck, and that will frighten them and force their hand."

The duke nodded, deep in thought. "I had not considered that possibility," he said slowly. "It is well thought on, ma'am."

"Understand that I would not put Anne in danger, your Grace, but I thought it might help to avoid bloodshed," she continued. "And if we can recover Melia without further alarums, so much the better."

He nodded again. "I certainly agree with you, ma'am. There have been quite enough alarums these past few hours, to say nothing of the past few weeks, to last me for the rest of my life."

The snap in that cold, drawling voice caused Anne to pull back on her side of the carriage and become a very small, very quiet young lady indeed.

8

"There they are," the duke said suddenly, breaking the silence that had fallen over the three of them as the carriage raced south. Juliet leaned forward and saw the outriders spurring their horses to surround a small cavalcade of brightly painted wagons with canvas tops, and a troop of swarthy men riding an odd miscellany of mounts. There were ill-groomed ponies and a burro, something that looked suspiciously like an old plow horse, and one handsome gray gelding. She was sure the rider of this horse must be the gypsies' leader, and it was by his side that the carriage drew to a halt. The man astride looked around at the grim faces of the duke's grooms and outriders and at the weapons in their hands, and his eyes gleamed. He was a short, stocky man with long black hair and a face that seemed to have been carved from teak. Juliet thought his head seemed much too large for his body, but even in the dirty, flamboyant clothes he wore, there was that about him that told you he was as proud and arrogant as the duke.

Juliet saw that the wagons had halted as commanded, and over the clinking of the harness and the snorts of the horses, she heard a strident, peremptory female voice call from one of the caravans. She did not understand the foreign dialect, but the tone of the woman's voice made it clear she was issuing a warning. For a moment, a look of anger crossed the leader's dark face, but then he edged his horse closer to the splendid carriage of the Duke of Severn. Juliet saw his eyes inspecting the shining equipage with its team of four matched blacks, and she was sure he did not miss the crest on the door.

"But how may we serve you, your Worship?" he

asked in English, his rough voice insolent. "You wish your fortunes told, perhaps?"

William Fairhaven stepped down from the carriage, and Anne cringed back in the far corner in fright. Juliet smiled at her to give her courage.

"You have something that belongs to me," the duke drawled. "Two things, to be precise. I want them back."

The gypsy shrugged and turned to speak in his own tongue at some length with his men. They began to laugh, and the duke's hand went to the pocket of his dark-blue coat. Juliet thought he looked magnificent, and frightening as well, he was so tall and assured. Not a hair was out of place under his fashionable beaver, and his linen gleamed white in the sunlight. His pale breeches clung without a wrinkle to his long, powerful legs, and his black boots shone. Compared to the ragged gypsies, he looked like a royal prince.

"But how can this be, sir?" the gypsy asked in a pitiful whine, and Juliet heard someone snicker. "As you can see, we are but a poor band of wanderers. What could we have that belongs to such as you?"

"Dismount, and give that order to your men," the duke commanded, his voice hard and cold.

For a moment, Juliet was sure the chief would refuse, for she saw his hands tighten on his reins. And then, once again, the hoarse female voice admonished him from the lead caravan, and he shrugged and called an order.

The other men dismounted and came to form a circle around their leader. Some women and ragged, barefoot children climbed out of the wagons to come and hold the men's horses. One of the women was very beautiful, and Juliet saw the way the men's eyes lingered on her handsome face with its full, red lips and dark, almond-shaped eyes. She was dressed in a tawdry yellow silk gown that obviously had known many other owners, although Juliet was sure none of them had ever filled it to such ripe, seductive perfection before. The chief gave her the reins of the gelding, and she took them with a toss of her head that set her waist-length black hair to swinging, and the gold loops in her ears to flash as they caught the light. Then her eyes went past the chief to where the duke stood, and she smiled and straightened her shoulders so her ripe, tip-tilted breasts were thrown into bold prominence.

The gypsy chief exclaimed and slapped her hard across the face. He barked an order, and she lowered her eyes and backed away, her unrepentent hips swaying. As soon as the chief turned away, her eyes sought the duke's again, and the glance she sent him was such a blatant invitation, so full of sexual meaning, that Juliet felt herself grow cold. She dragged her eyes back to the two protagonists before her.

"Now, your Worship, if you would describe these things you claim are yours?" the gypsy leader asked, his hands on his hips. He had to look a long way up at the duke, and it did not seem to please him.

The duke smiled, but it was not a smile that reassured the men who were standing before him, never taking their dark eyes from his. "I can do even better than that," he said, and he added without turning his head, "Come here, Anne."

Juliet sent the girl a glance of encouragement, and she was glad to see her put her chin up before she slid along the seat and stepped out into the dusty road. There was a gasp as she climbed down and went to stand beside her father. Some of the gypsies backed away, and from the caravans and the circle of children, an excited, frightened chatter arose. The chief stepped away and made a gesture with his hands, as if to ward off something evil, and then Juliet saw him look quickly to the lead wagon. She was sure that that was where Amelia was being held captive. The duke noticed it too, for he motioned to two of the grooms. The men moved forward. From the lead wagon, a wailing voice began to croon some wordless incantation that seemed to recount misery, dark deeds, and endless malediction. Juliet knew it was the saddest, most frightening thing she had heard in a long, long time. When the voice died away at last, it took a major effort for her to loosen her tightly clasped hands.

"What I seek, you see before you," the duke said into the sudden silence. "Release the girl at once."

The chief stood still, staring at Anne in horror, and then he barked an order. The flap of canvas at the back of the first caravan opened slowly, and Amelia climbed down. The gypsies gasped again, and many of them cried out in fear as she came to stand beside her twin. Dressed in the same shirt and breeches, it was uncanny how much they resembled each other.

"Oh, Father, I am so glad you—" Amelia began, but the duke interrupted her harshly.

"Be silent!" he thundered, and she paled and took Anne's hand in a tight grasp.

The duke turned to the gypsy leader. "It only remains for you to return the horse you stole, and we will be on our way," he said, his voice deceptively mild now.

"You will let us go?" the chief asked as if he could not believe his ears.

"Why should I detain you?" the duke asked. "I can assure you I have no more desire for any more of your company, and one can hardly blame you for taking what fell into your hands like a ripe plum."

The chief nodded, and then his gaze went back to where the two young girls stood hand in hand, and once again he made that motion of fear. Juliet had seen her uncle's slaves make a gesture very much like it when they were afraid of voodoo.

The chief turned his head and spoke rapidly in Romany. One of the men began to argue, and the chief whirled, a long thin knife Juliet had not even suspected he carried, clutched in his hand. As he flourished it, the other gypsy stopped protesting at once and motioned one of the children to bring the old plow horse forward. Juliet looked to the duke, wondering if he would bother to take possession of such a tired, decrepit animal. Perhaps this Mr. Harden might even be appeased if he was presented with a new, young horse, she thought.

The duke's face seemed made of stone as he looked the band over, one by one. His glance lingered for only a moment on the handsome gypsy girl who held the gelding, and then he turned to inspect the plow horse.

"This is Mr. Harden's horse?" he asked, not looking at the twins.

"Yes, Father," both girls answered in unison, loosing another flood of excited conjecture and cries of fright.

"As a reward for returning my daughter to me, I will give you the horse," the duke told the head gypsy.

The chief did not look at all pleased now. Perhaps he did not want anything to do with an animal the twins had touched and ridden, Juliet thought. The duke motioned to his daughters. "Get into the carriage," he ordered in his slow drawl, and they backed away, guarded by the grooms.

The duke waited until they were safely seated before he called to his men and then turned to follow them.

Suddenly the gypsy said in a voice full of awe, "It is a thousand pities, your Worship, that you are so afflicted, but that you should seek to get your bad luck back amazes me. You should have killed one of them at birth. Women are worthless creatures, good for very little. Why saddle yourself with such a curse?"

One booted foot on the step, the duke turned back to stare at his daughter's abductor. "You will never know how cursed I am," he said, his voice slow and emotionless. "I discover new proof of it every day."

The gypsy nodded in sympathy, but he did not speak again or try to detain them further. He seemed to be willing them to be gone, carrying the twins with them. Juliet sensed he would put as much distance as he could between them before he allowed the band to stop and camp again.

One of the grooms shut the door behind the duke, and he settled back on the squabs before he gave the office to start. He stared out the window at the gypsies, ignoring Anne and Amelia as if he had not spent the better part of the day searching for them at all. Juliet saw that their faces were identically white and frightened and that they were huddled close together, as if the contact gave them courage. She looked especially hard at Amelia, but to her relief she saw no lingering horror in her eyes, no new knowledge that at her age she should not have had to learn.

There was no conversation as the carriage rumbled back at a much slower pace to Eggesford. The duke stared out the window beside him, one shapely hand caressing his chin as if he were deep in thought. Neither of the girls showed any desire to interrupt his musing, and Juliet applauded their tact. She had sent Amelia a warm glance of relief, but outside of a tremulous smile, so quickly gone she thought she must have imagined it, neither girl caught her eye again.

The carriage had come to a stop in the yard of the Blue Boar Inn before the duke broke the silence at last. "We will stop here for something to eat and drink, and so the Lady Juliet can rest," he said. "This has been a most upsetting experience for her, as it has been for me. Fortunately, no one knows me here, so your *outré* appearance will occasion no comment."

His dark eyes inspected his daughters without expression. "And then we shall return to Severn. I do not care to speak to either of you until we reach there, is that understood?"

The girls nodded, mute still, and he stepped down to

offer his arm to Juliet, leaving them to follow like the two young boys they appeared.

Juliet saw he must have made arrangements earlier, for the inkeeper bowed them to his best private parlor at once. The duke stood aside so his daughters could enter, and then he put a deterring hand on Juliet's arm. She looked up into his stern face, so concerned for the twins that she did not even notice his unwelcome touch.

"A few moments of your time in private, m'lady, if you would be so good," he murmured, gesturing toward another parlor a little way down the hall. Juliet bit her lip and nodded, and he closed the door behind his daughters and led her away.

When he had seated her before the fire, he began to stride up and down. Bewildered, Juliet watched him, wondering what was troubling him. Before she could speak, he said, "Someone must speak to the twins while they are still frightened and contrite. I am not the best person to do it. May I beg your assistance once more, ma'am?"

Juliet nodded, her hazel eyes confused. Surely the duke would have no trouble finding the cutting words and icy phrases to chastise his daughters. Why did he ask her to do it for him?

He came to stand before her then, and he leaned down and put both hands on the arms of her chair, his dark eyes searching her hazel ones as he tried to tell her what he wanted. "It must be explained to them, in very precise and realistic words, exactly what could have happened to them while they were unprotected and away from Severn. For the danger was not only from the gypsy men, but from any tinker or farmhand they chanced to meet. Their age and disguise protected them this time. Next time they might not be so lucky. Forgive me for speaking plainly, Lady Juliet, but I want them to know how horrible rape is, so they will never again take

103

the risks they did with this adventure, and I want them to know it now, while this episode is still vivid in their minds. I am sure you can see why my speaking of it would only embarrass them, but coming from a woman and a friend will alleviate the shock."

"No!" Juliet cried, throwing out her hands in revulsion.

The duke straightened up in his astonishment. "No?" he asked. "Surely you can see that this is one subject their father cannot discuss with them."

"I know you can't, you shouldn't," Juliet said wildly, and she rose to stride up and down in turn. Then she took a deep breath. "But I cannot do it either. Do not ask it of me, your Grace, I beg you."

William Fairhaven stared down into her pale face. He saw the distress deep in her hazel eyes, and he bowed over her hand. "Very well, I shall not ask it of you, ma'am," he said, trying to keep his voice calm and re-assuring. "You have done so much for the twins already, it was not fair of me to expect you to compromise your standards as a lady. After all, you are not married, but I forgot that in my duress. Forgive me. I shall have my housekeeper, Mrs. Pomfret, talk to them when we return to Severn."

Juliet was glad he had spoken as he had, for she was all too aware that she had let down her guard for a moment and told the duke more than she ever wanted him to know.

"Thank you," she said in a little voice.

"I will stay here in this room," the duke went on, his voice casual. "I meant it when I said I did not care to speak to the twins until we reach Severn. You see, I am so afraid that when I rip up at them for their willful disobedience, I might lose my temper and be tempted to do the murder the gypsy suggested. And not to just one of them, Lady Juliet, but to both. I have never known such maddening females. They are impossible!"

Juliet tried to smile. "I think that is a wise course, sir. It will be easier for them to eat and rest if you are not present. You have a most lowering affect on them, your Grace," she said.

The duke looked down at her, one eyebrow quirked as he led her to the door. "Can it be that you are still bemoaning the loss of their vivacity and charm, ma'am? Even after this escapade?"

"No, I am not," Juliet said tartly. "At the moment, I am tempted to give them a tongue-lashing myself, and I pray you do not put any whips in *my* way."

The duke laughed, and then he bowed as they reached the private parlor he had engaged. "We shall leave for Severn in an hour, ma'am. Until I can reinforce my displeasure with suitably black looks and a frozen silence, I beg you to hold firm to that resolution. No sympathy now, no petting and consoling them. We must let them know they have been very, very bad. I can rely on you for that, at least, I am sure."

Juliet curtsied as he opened the door for her, and she murmured as she crossed in front of him, "On that point you may be easy, your Grace. I shall not fail you."

She was proud of her self-control and the light way she had recovered herself, and she was sure that the duke had come to see that her abhorrence of speaking of sexual matters to the twins was only a maidenly reluctance and reserve.

She could not know that, as William Fairhaven ate his solitary repast, he did not think of his daughters first. Instead, he pondered the puzzle that was the Lady Juliet Manchester, and tried to imagine what had happened to her that had made her the cold, proper lady she was. At thirty-one she was no child, and even if he had been remiss in asking her to speak of such things openly, surely she was enough a woman of the world to be able to warn the girls in such a way that they would never again be so careless. He had not expected her to be clinical; what he had hoped was that she would be able to make them fearful and more inclined to caution, for what a woman gave freely to a man she loved could in no way compare to the brutal possession of a strange man who had no concern for his victim. He prayed God his daughters would never know such pain and degradation, and he promised himself that if Mrs. Pomfret also refused that task, he would have to take it upon himself to tell them about it. They were so young, so innocent and fresh. He could never bear it if that innocence was defiled.

The duke poured himself another glass of wine. He was somewhat amazed at the intensity of his feelings, for never before had he spent much time thinking of the twins and all the pitfalls they might face along life's pathway. But today he had been ready to do murder if he had discovered Amelia had been harmed by the gypsy band. He smiled a little grimly. It appeared that he, who always up to this point had scorned fatherhood and all its ramifications, had suddenly embraced it with an intensity that was quite foreign to him.

In the private parlor down the hallway, the Ladies Anne and Amelia were regaling Juliet with a breathless account of their adventure. Juliet had scolded them and shown her disappointment in their behavior as best she could, and both girls had promised her they would never do such a thing again.

"For it was so frightening, m'lady," Anne told her, her blue eyes wide. "When they dragged Melia into the caravan, I had all I could do not to rush to her rescue at once."

"But we had a pact," Amelia continued as her twin paused for breath. "If I were in any danger, Anne was to take the horse and ride for help. Truly, dear Juliet, we never thought there would be any risk at all."

Juliet longed to shake them both. For one brief

moment, she toyed with the idea of mentioning the rape the duke had asked her to speak about, but she could not bring herself to do it. Instead, she said, "But of course, by the time Anne reached Eggesford, or even the nearest farm on that horrible old horse, it might have been much, much too late."

Both girls looked thoughtful, and then Anne pressed the last bun on her sister. "You must be starving, Melia," she said. "Did they give you anything to eat at all?"

"Only a kind of maize pudding," Amelia admitted as she accepted the bun. "It had garlic in it."

"For breakfast?" Anne asked as if she could not believe such a thing.

"And tonight they were going to bake a hedgehog," Amelia said, spreading her bun lavishly with jam.

"Ugh! How glad I am Father came after us before you had to eat that," her twin said with a shudder. "And you too, of course, Juliet. It is always so much easier when you are with us."

"Did you and Father have a nice drive here, ma'am?" Amelia inquired through the large mouthful of bun she had taken.

Juliet put down her teacup. "Of course we did not! We were not out for a jaunt in the country, you know, and we were much too concerned about you to enjoy ourselves."

Anne kicked her twin under the table. "Father is such a good-looking man, isn't he?" she asked Juliet. "I never thought so before, but when I saw him among all those dirty little gypsy men, I could not help but compare him, so tall and elegant, and—and so much in command."

"Oh, yes," Amelia agreed fervently, in clearer accents now she had disposed of the bun. "He was wonderful, don't you agree, Juliet?"

Juliet poured them all another cup of tea, frowning a

little as she did so. "Hmm?" she asked as if she had been thinking of something else. To herself, she admitted the duke *had* been wonderful, for she knew that even without the surprise of Anne as an extra arrow in his quiver, he would have won through easily. She could not imagine him failing at anything he set out to do.

"That gypsy girl thought so too," Anne continued, taking the cup Juliet handed her. "The pretty one in the tight yellow dress, I mean. Did you see the way she looked at Father?"

Amelia looked thoughtful. "She stared at him just the way Mrs. Kingley used to do, remember, Anne?"

Her twin giggled. "Yes, you're right! Mrs. Kingley always reminded me of the way the cook's cat looks when he catches a mouse. So sleek and pleased and— and hungry!"

Juliet longed to ask who this voracious Mrs. Kingley was, but she made herself sit quietly and sip her tea.

"It was plain to see that the gypsy chief didn't care for her looking at Father, though," Anne went on. "How hard he slapped her! Do they do that often, Melia?"

"More often than not. And they are so strange," Amelia said. "The old woman who kept me prisoner is like a queen. She tells everyone what to do, even that nasty chief. She's like a—a maytrack."

"Matriarch," Juliet corrected.

"She was the one who said they should sell me, for she claimed I would bring them bad luck," Amelia continued. "But then she read my palm."

Anne put down her cup, her eyes shining in anticipation. "What did she say, twin?" she asked breathlessly.

Amelia colored up. "Some of it was silly and made no sense at all," she reported. "She said I would have a happy marriage someday and have many children. She wouldn't tell me if my husband will be handsome or kind, just that he will be an unusual man. How silly! And then she said there were going to be a lot of changes in my life, starting almost at once. She said I would leave home—well, I had already done so, hadn't I?—and that there was a fair lady and a dark man in my future, and many storms ahead." Amelia shrugged. "I expect she says much the same to everyone."

"No, no, twin, you're not thinking," Anne exclaimed. "The dark man must be Father, and the fair lady Juliet."

She stopped speaking suddenly, as if she had just remembered the company they were in, and Juliet laughed. "But I am already in your lives, my dears, as is your father. However, she had better not be right in predicting any more storms, or about your leaving home. You must never do so again, let me tell you! Your father's patience is wearing thin."

Before the girls could answer, there was a rap on the door and the duke's cold voice telling them the carriage was waiting to take them home to Severn.

As Juliet began to gather up her things, she missed the little smile and satisfied nod the twins exchanged, as if their adventure had more than fulfilled their expectations.

9

By the time the duke's carriage left her at the manse, Lady Juliet was delighted to take her leave of the Fairhaven family. The journey had been difficult, for outside of a few commonplace remarks to her, the duke had maintained the frozen silence he had promised. In the face of his black looks and obvious disapproval, the twins had remained silent as well.

As Juliet made her way up the stairs to her room, she told herself that the only good part of the return to Severn had been the complete absence of the duke's former teasing and lovemaking. She wished with all her heart that she did not have to see him ever again. Would he never leave Devon?

At dinner, after the maid had been dismissed, she regaled her brother with an account of her day. It would not do for Phyllis to hear anything, for then it would be all over the village in a matter of minutes.

As she suspected, Romeo not only frowned, but chuckled as well. "Why, I am sure that even in London there is not such a drama being enacted on the stage, my dear," he told her. "Runaways! Gypsies! A dash to the rescue!"

"Perhaps not," Juliet agreed, finishing her pudding. "And yet, what happens on the stage is much less traumatic than when it occurs in real life. The twins have been very remiss and naughty. I hope the duke punishes them for it accordingly, although I pray he will refrain from beating them."

"He does not look like a man given to corporal punishment," the vicar remarked. "There is a kindness in his eyes that he tries very hard to hide. Haven't you noticed it? No, no, his retaliation will take another form."

Juliet was struck by a sudden idea. "Romeo, I have been thinking," she said slowly, pleating her napkin in restless fingers.

Her brother looked inquiring, and she continued, "I do believe I will go up to London, after all. It is September now, and there is all the Little Season to enjoy. I think I shall write to Aunt Elizabeth tomorrow."

The vicar beamed. "I am so glad, dear," he exclaimed. "Now you will be able to see all the new plays and operas, and enjoy the balls and parties and other social events while you wear your pretty gowns."

Juliet rose from the table before he could begin to enumerate the other treats in store, treats that were sure to lead eventually down a church aisle on the arm of some handsome, smitten peer.

The following morning she wrote her letter, and then, feeling restless, she decided to go riding. She had not done so recently, for she felt a little reluctance to trespass on the duke's land while he was in residence. Today, however, she could do so with impunity. The duke would never know, for he was sure to be overseeing his daughters' punishment.

Besides, she needed to be alone so she could think. She had felt calmer after she announced her decision to go to town, but she had had trouble getting to sleep later that evening. The duke's dark face kept appearing in her mind, and his teasing, drawling words kept echoing in her ears. She seemed to keep hearing him say that she was to be his concern, that there was something between them, something that would grow into a wondrous, consuming thing, that he was determined on her capitulation. She had turned over and pounded her pillow, as if by that action she could banish him from her thoughts, but it was a long time before she went to sleep.

She sent an order to the stable, and then she donned a dark-green habit and broad-brimmed hat adorned with long, colorful feathers.

After she was mounted, she followed the post road for a mile or so, and then she cut across one of the duke's fields to the park beyond. She knew she could not be seen from the hall, and she did not expect to meet anyone in this lonely part of the estate. The morning was full of bright sunlight, and there was a little breeze and just enough of a bite in the air to tell you that winter was coming to displace summer yet again.

As she rode, she wondered how the twins were faring and what punishment the duke had set them. In a way, she wished she might have listened in on the lecture he must have given them. He would not have ranted or raved at them or raised his voice, she knew, for that was not William Fairhaven's style. No. Instead, he would have frozen them with icy words and sarcastic denunciations that would have them both squirming with embarrassment and chagrin. And then, when he had them humble and on the verge of tears, he would order them to some onerous chore as payment for worrying him. And Juliet knew the duke had been worried. She had seen the extent of it on his face in his relief at finding Anne and after his subsequent rescue of Amelia.

Juliet would have been amazed at the way William Fairhaven did handle the situation.

When the carriage reached Severn and before any of them alighted, the duke spoke to his daughters for the first time. He ordered them to their rooms for a bath and a change of clothes. They were to eat a solitary supper on trays there and present themselves in his library at nine that evening. Until that time, they were not to leave their rooms for any reason whatsoever, unless he himself ordered them to do so in the unlikely event that Severn was engulfed in flames.

He glared at them as he spoke, his dark eyes burning into theirs as he asked them if they quite understood his orders. Anne and Amelia nodded, looking frightened. He noticed that Anne did not even tilt her chin at him as was her custom, and Amelia appeared completely subdued.

After he had seen the girls scurry up the stairs, the duke went to the library and called for his housekeeper to apprise her of the situation and ask her help. But although Mrs. Pomfret was shocked at the young ladies' behavior, she refused to speak to them about men, much to the duke's surprise.

112

"Begging your pardon, your Grace," she said, her usual stately accents sounding slightly ruffled, "but I could not bring myself to do so. Why, every feeling must be offended." Two red spots appeared on her sallow cheeks as she added, "I am not really 'Mrs.' Pomfret. That is a courtesy title because I am housekeeper here. So you see, I—I would not have any idea what to say to them."

The duke excused her abruptly before he was tempted to laugh. How many reluctant virgins he had had to deal with today, he thought. Lady Juliet's unwillingness at least was understandable, but for Mrs. Pomfret—or Miss Pomfret, as he now knew her to be—who must be sixty if she was a day, to claim shyness and ignorance was ridiculous. He sighed and went to eat his lonely dinner while he pondered this new problem.

When the twins came to stand before him and curtsy as the library clock was chiming the first stroke of the hour, he was ready. As ready as I'll ever be, he told himself with grim determination. They were dressed all in white, their black hair held back by bands of white ribbon before it flowed down their backs. Their faces were as colorless as their gowns. He was sure Anne had hit on the scheme to dress as two innocent lambs in order to gain sympathy, and his eyes grew colder. The Lady Anne was as clever as she could stare, and had a definite bent for dramatization, but she would discover her father was onto all her tricks.

"How much more suitable your attire is now, my dear twins," he drawled as he motioned them to take a seat. "Although I must say I think the effect of two young girls dressed as if they were about to be forced into a tumbril for the ride to the guillotine is a bit overdone in this instance."

Amelia bit her lip at his dry sarcasm and for a moment gave her twin a burning glance of reproach. Anne flushed crimson.

The duke spoke uninterrupted for several minutes. The twins had heard many lectures from him before, but this one surpassed them all in causticity, denunciation, and icy disapproval. He did not raise his voice, but his words were succinct and determined, and before very long they were both wishing he would beat them instead.

And then he paused to glower at them, and there was silence at last in the large room. The duke went to stare down into the fire, one foot on the fender as he leaned on the mantel, deep in thought. The twins exchanged frightened glances, and Anne silently warned her sister their punishment was coming.

But the words that their father uttered next were completely unexpected. He asked them in a quiet voice what they knew about men and about their own sex. For a moment, stunned by the change of subject, they remained silent, and then Anne asked, "Do you mean how babies come, Father?"

The duke nodded.

"Oh, we know all about that, don't we, Melia?" she said, little knowing the relief that flooded her father's breast at her airy words. "Why do you ask?"

"Who told you?" the duke demanded, remembering Mrs. Pomfret's strict notions. Perhaps one of their governesses had been more enlightened than most, he thought, wishing he had given her a more munificent salary.

"Why, Will did," Amelia spoke up.

The duke's black brows soared. "Your brother? How did he come to do so?" he asked, his voice harsh now.

"It was last spring," Anne said, taking up the tale as Melia cringed back in her chair. "He said it was just an ordinary part of life and it was ridiculous that we were so ignorant, didn't he, Melia? It was when one of the mares foaled and he found out we didn't have any idea

114

how it had happened. He took us to one of the farms so we could see a stallion and a mare ourselves."

The duke realized there was more to his heir than he had ever imagined, and he looked forward to getting to know him better.

"I thought it was funny—so awkward," Amelia volunteered.

"Will told us that it was different for people and that when we were older we would understand it better," Anne went on. "But I do not think I will ever like it, no matter what he says," she added naïvely.

"Nor I," Amelia agreed.

The duke saw his opening and was quick to take it. "Then you must be more careful in the future, daughters. What you did when you ran away could have led to a more intimate knowledge of sexual matters than you should know at this time."

He paused to see his daughters staring at him in disbelief, and he made himself continue in a calm, sure voice, "Men are not always kind or good. Some of them force women—girls—to intimacy. It is called 'rape' and it is something I pray sincerely you will never know. But you have a responsibility too. You must never permit yourselves to get into a situation where rape is possible, if you can avoid it. By leaving Severn, even dressed as boys, you invited that possibility. It was quite the worst part of your disobedience and it worried me very much."

"But we are not old enough, Father. Why, we are only thirteen," Anne said indignantly. "Surely a man would not touch us!"

The duke shook his head. "You are very young and immature, that is true, Anne, but that would not make a difference to some men."

"How awful," Amelia exclaimed.

The duke felt he had more than gotten his point

across, and not wanting them to feel any revulsion for what could be such a wonderful thing, he said, "We will not speak of it again. When you are older and fall in love and marry, you will discover that the act of love-making is not only beautiful and fulfilling, but that you will enjoy it very much."

He saw that they both looked unconvinced, and he added, "You have my promise on it. I know."

The twins nodded, and William Fairhaven took a deep breath. He had been glad they had shown no embarrassment at his explanation, and he thought he had muddled through it very well, with the help of his absent heir, but he was glad that it was over. If only their mother had lived, he would never have been put to such a task, he knew, but it had come out better than he had expected.

"That will be all," he said now in dismissal.

The twins stood up and exchanged confused glances. "But—but what is to be our punishment, Father?" Anne asked bravely.

"Aren't you going to beat us?" Amelia whispered.

The duke did not smile as he looked down at the two of them, so slender and frightened, and yet standing as straight and as bravely as two soldiers waiting to be disciplined. He reached out and put an arm around them both, feeling that now-familiar constriction in his throat.

"When have I ever beaten you?" he asked in his usual drawl.

He felt the girls move closer, and then they put their arms around his waist. As he walked them to the door, he added, "There would be no sense in it, not now. I should have done it the minute I saw you when I was in such a white heat of rage. I cannot do it now in cold blood."

"But aren't we going to have to write some long essay

or read some tiresome book of sermons?'' Anne persisted.

The duke, who had been thinking of presenting them with just such a task, found wisdom. ''No, you are not,'' he told them, and then he stopped and stood them both in front of him so he could look down into their eyes.

''Your punishment is that you shall have none at all,'' he said. The twins' eyes grew wide with surprise. ''Instead, I leave it to you, as the Ladies Anne and Amelia Fairhaven, to think about the wrong you have done. I know you consider me overproud of our name, but we come from a great and noble family that has descended in an upbroken line for centuries. As such, much more is expected of all of us than is required of ordinary people. We have a heritage to maintain—and maintain well.''

He paused and looked searchingly into their eyes. ''I hope you will reflect on how much you have distressed everyone here at Severn, all these people who look up to you and care for you and who have a right to expect much better from their young ladies. And I want you to ponder how you angered and worried me. and your good friend the Lady Juliet as well.''

The twins looked stunned and, he thought, almost disappointed at his quiet words, and he realized that he had hit on the most crushing penance he could ever have devised. Beginning to know his daughters as he did, he knew it would be a long time before they would forget this adventure.

After they had left him, he went to pour himself a congratulatory snifter of brandy, feeling much more at ease. Indeed, he thought as he took his seat before the fire, it would not be too much to say that he was proud of the competent way he had handled the situation.

Fatherhood was not so difficult, after all. Why, it appeared he had a genuine aptitude for it!

The duke slept well that night, and he rose earlier than was his custom, breakfasting alone before he ordered a horse to be brought up from the stables. He had decided he would not seek the twins out, but would leave them to their own devices. They would be amazed at the relaxation of his supervision, and he was anxious to see how they would handle it. Somehow he did not think they would abuse their new freedom—not today, anyway, and perhaps not for some time to come.

He rode over his acres for over an hour, enjoying the crisp morning and the clear air. He would have been the first to say that his stay in the country was growing tedious, but he had to admit that mornings such as this, spent on horseback, did much to alleviate his boredom.

And then, in the distance, he spotted another rider. She was dressed in green and cantering along a ridge on a chestnut mare. As the sunlight lit her ash-blond hair with golden highlights, he knew it was Lady Juliet, and he spurred his horse to a gallop to intercept her.

Juliet heard the thundering hooves behind her and, suspecting who the rider might be, was tempted to urge her mare to a faster pace. But she held the canter, for she realized the duke would probably catch her with ease, and she did not want to give the appearance of flight.

When he came up beside her, she turned and smiled coolly as she reined in the mare. The duke halted his horse as well, and transferring his reins to one gloved hand, he swept his hat from his smooth dark hair and bowed to her over the saddle.

"Good morning, Lady Juliet," he drawled, his wicked smile showing his delight at their confrontation.

Juliet made herself smile again in return as she murmured, "Good morning, your Grace."

"A lovely day for a ride, is it not?" he asked next.

"It is, but even so, I am surprised to find you abroad, sir," Juliet told him. At his look of inquiry, she explained, "I was sure you would be very much occupied with the twins this morning."

"Supervising the installation of new chains in the dungeon where they are to be imprisoned, ma'am?" he asked innocently. "I can assure you I am not so harsh."

Then as his horse snorted and sidled, he asked, "Shall we walk them?"

Juliet nodded and braced herself for a further battle of wits with the Dreadful Duke.

"If I were so cruel, you might well find yourself chained next to them," he continued. "After all, I have caught you in the very act, fair trespasser."

"I admit a long-standing guilt. I have been riding your land for well over a year, sir," she replied. "However, I beg you for mercy. Please do not chain me in your dungeon. They are generally so damp, are they not?"

She saw a dangerous twinkle in his eye, and before he could say whatever outrageous thing had come into his mind, she asked, "Does Severn have a dungeon, by the way?"

"No, it does not," he answered. "If there were one, you may be sure the Ladies Anne and Amelia would have found some way to use it before now. Probably to incarcerate me there, by some wile."

Juliet found herself chuckling, and then she asked, "What was their explanation for running away to the gypsies, your Grace?"

The duke frowned a little. "Do you know, I never thought to ask them. You remind me I have been most remiss."

"And are they hard at work this morning at some difficult task you have set them?" she asked next, pleased at the way the meeting was going.

The duke laughed. Juliet thought he seemed more carefree today than he ever had before. "I have no idea what they are doing," he said. "You see, dear ma'am, I did not beat them or set them any punishment at all. All they had to endure was a tongue-lashing." He paused, and then he added pensively, "Although I am held to be rather expert at giving those, you know."

"No punishment at all?" Juliet asked in amazement.

The duke explained what he had done, and Juliet found herself applauding his astuteness.

"Unfortunately," he went on smoothly, "like you, my housekeeper did not feel able to discuss that subject I was so anxious for the twins to learn."

Juliet turned to stare at him, but when she saw the amused quirk of his lips and the devilish gleam in his eyes, she turned away in haste. "Indeed?" she asked through suddenly stiff lips.

"It turns out that 'Mrs.' Pomfret is a spinster and, as such, was forced to demur, claiming ignorance. I find it hard to imagine how she could have reached such a venerable age in the virginal state, but let that go." He paused for a moment, and then he continued, "You are not to worry about the twins' lack of knowledge, m'lady. I took on the task myself and managed to scrape through it tolerably well, all thanks to some inadvertent help from my eldest son."

Juliet did not know what he was talking about, but she had no intention of inquiring and she was glad to find they had reached a fork in the bridle path. She halted her mare and tightened her hands on the reins as she said, "This is where we part, your Grace. I must return to the manse, and it lies in quite the opposite direction from the hall at this point."

"But I cannot allow you to, er, shall we say *escape* me? so quickly, ma'am," the duke told her, and her heart sank. "Come, you must join me and the twins for a luncheon before you return home."

Juliet was about to refuse when he added, "Surely you would not miss the opportunity to see for yourself that Anne and Amelia are none the worse for their adventure, and when they see you with me, they will know that they did not dream my restraint, for everything will be as usual."

Juliet could think of no excuse that would not sound rude. "Thank you, that would be delightful," she said as easily as she could, wheeling her mare in the direction of Severn.

As they rode toward the hall, she kept up a light conversation on various innocuous subjects. She was glad the duke followed her lead, but she thought she detected amusement in his expression and polite replies.

She was relieved when they rode up to the front of the hall and grooms came running to take their mounts in charge. And then she realized that the duke was coming around to help her dismount, and she loosened her foot from the stirrup and prepared to slide down herself.

In her haste to escape his touch, the train of her habit got tangled in her spur and she would have fallen if the duke had not caught her up in his arms.

"My dear Lady Juliet," he said calmly in his slow drawl as he bent over her, "you must have a better care of yourself."

His dark face was so near to hers that Juliet felt almost ill. She could feel his strong arms holding her close to his chest, one arm around her waist and the other under her thighs, and her heart began to pound. He tightened his grasp while he leisurely inspected her face, a little smile curling his lips.

The grooms were leading the horses away, but still she demanded to be put down at once in a frantic whisper, for her mouth was dry with fear.

For a moment, she thought he would refuse, but then he stood her on her feet. She tried to step away, but once again her train betrayed her and she stumbled. The duke's arms came back around her waist to hold her safe, and he murmured, "You are having a time of it, are you not? I never realized trains could be such troublesome things. It is too bad."

Juliet twisted out of his grasp and reached down to pick up the offending material, wishing she could rip it off her habit right here. She was speechless and trembling with fury—at the duke, at her clumsiness, at this whole uncomfortable situation.

"How handsome you are when you are angry, m'lady," the duke complimented her as he held out his arm to help her up the steps. "Your eyes sparkle with the same gold that threads through your hair, and I am sure there isn't a single rose in Severn's gardens that could rival the ones in your cheeks."

Juliet threw him a glance that spoke volumes, and ignored his arm as she put up her chin and marched up the steps, her lips set tight. Never had the long flight seemed longer. The duke walked beside her, matching her step for step, his dark eyes gleaming with amusement at her predicament.

Up in the schoolroom, the twins watched them with glee, and when the pair had disappeared under the massive portico with its hundred-foot pillars, they seized each other and began a mad, congratulatory whirl around the schoolroom, scattering books and papers with reckless abandon.

As the duke and Lady Juliet entered the main hall, they found the butler directing two of the footmen in the unpacking of a large crate.

"This has just arrived from London, your Grace," Devett told him. "I believe it is your portrait, sir." He handed the duke a letter and then turned back to supervise the footmen.

The duke asked permission to read his note, by raising his brows at Juliet, and she nodded. She was glad to have a moment to calm herself, she realized, and she concentrated on breathing slowly until the color in her hot cheeks had time to fade.

She heard the duke's chuckle, and she looked up to see him smiling in genuine amusement as he finished his letter.

"But I must have your opinion, Lady Juliet," he said, waving toward the crate. The footmen had removed the last nails and were carefully lifting the huge gold-framed canvas from its hiding place, to unwrap it from the cloths that protected it.

As the painting came to light, Juliet found herself face to face with her nemesis, and her heart, so carefully returned to a normal beat, began to pound anew as she stared at that tall, masculine figure with its handsome face and alert dark eyes. She could not seem to make herself look away from it.

"What do you think of it, ma'am?" the duke inquired from close beside her, startling her considerably. "I admit I am more than pleased with it myself."

"It is most faithful to you, sir, and very well executed," she told him as the footmen bundled up the packing material to remove it from the hall. "Who was the artist?" she asked next. She was sure William Fairhaven was waiting for a more effusive reply, and she was determined he should not have one.

"A woman. A very talented woman that it is my great privilege to know," the duke told her, staring at the portrait and then at the letter in his hand. For a moment, she thought she saw a look of regret come over his face, and she wondered who this talented woman was and how well he knew her.

"Her name is Claire Tyson," the duke told her as if he had read her mind.

And then, they both heard the twins clattering down the marble stairs from the third-floor schoolroom. They waited together, looking up the flight in anticipation, the duke with regret that his daughters had appeared so soon, and Lady Juliet in profound relief that their tête-á-tête had ended at last.

10

Luncheon, which might have been awkward with all the undercurrents that were flowing between the four participants, was saved by the arrival of the duke's portrait.

The twins exclaimed over it, asking Juliet's agreement with their lavish praise so many times that she had all she could do to remain calm and detached. The duke stood by, his manner amused, as if he knew very well how much she disliked the position she found herself in, of having to compliment him. Juliet wished she might tell him exactly what she thought of him instead.

"Shall you put it in the north gallery with all the other dukes and duchesses, Father?" Anne asked.

"I had not considered where it should hang. What do you suggest?" he asked as he ushered them to the morning room, where luncheon was to be served.

"Oh, let's not put it way off up there," Amelia said. "It would be such a waste, for hardly anybody ever goes there."

"We went this morning," Anne reminded her as she took her seat.

"But that was just to inspect our ancestors," Amelia said, and then she stole a scared little glance at her father. He smiled at her as he sat down, looking pleased that his lecture the evening before had prompted the twins' visit to the gallery.

"I think it should go in the great hall, in place of one

of those murky old landscapes," Anne said next. "After all, you are the current duke. Why shouldn't you have the place of honor?"

"That is well thought on, my dear," the duke told her. "I agree, but for quite another reason."

The girls looked inquiring and he explained, "That way, even when I am not in residence at Severn, you will have to pass it every day, and it might remind you to behave yourselves."

"Father!" both twins cried in unison, and Juliet had to smile in spite of herself. She was amazed at the rapport between the three Fairhavens and how easy the twins were now in their father's company.

"I wonder if it is very hard to learn to paint like that?" Amelia pondered as she took a portion of the game pie the footman was presenting.

"It takes a long time, Melia," the duke said. "Many years of serious work. Lady Blagdon, the artist who painted it, has been studying since she was your age."

"Was it really done by a woman, Father?" Anne asked in stunned accents. "And she a lady? How very unusual!"

"I believe women are able to do many things," Juliet said. Then she wished she had not spoken, as all eyes turned her way.

"You are correct, ma'am," the duke agreed calmly. "If Lady Blagdon is to be believed, women are not helpless, mindless creatures incapable of serious endeavor, for that is only a myth put about by men. She has always considered the feminine sex to be the equals of men in talent and intelligence."

"I should like to meet her very much," Anne said, speaking Juliet's own thought aloud. "She sounds so unique."

"And I," Amelia agreed. "I have never done any serious painting, just pencil sketches, but I would like to ask her about them. How wonderful it must be to be able to paint like that!''

Her voice was so admiring and so wistful that the duke paused, his wineglass half-lifted to his mouth. ''And so you shall, Melia,'' he promised her, and was delighted at the way the twins' blue eyes lit up. ''At the moment, Claire cannot travel or entertain, for she is expecting her third child, but perhaps next spring we will ask her to come to Severn. And of course, her husband, the marquess. You will like him too. Claire and Andrew Tyson are my very good friends.''

Juliet wondered why this pronouncement lightened her mood.

Conversation became more general then and ranged over a number of subjects. Juliet was glad the twins were so talkative, for it kept the duke's attention from her and allowed her to leave the center of the stage. Anne even teased him a little, drawing a smile to his lips when she told him how much more ducal he was than some of the former rulers of Severn, and his eyes grew noticeably softer when Amelia exclaimed, ''And so much handsomer, too!''

Even when the duke thought to ask the twins why they had run off to the gypsies, the atmosphere remained light. The girls did exchange a glance, for they knew they could not mention that Juliet's refusal of two invitations to Severn had made them do it to force her into their father's company. Instead, Anne said she had never seen any gypsies, and Amelia claimed they had wanted their fortunes told the very worst way. The duke shook his head at these reasons, but he forbore to scold them further.

Juliet was almost enjoying herself when the duke turned to her and asked her to tell him about her life in America. For a moment, she did not know what to say, and she was glad to have the little respite the twins gave her as they begged, "Do tell Father some of your adventures, Juliet!"

"Tell him about the riverboats, and the plantation—"

"Those huge oaks dripping with moss, and the way the sugarcane fields looked at harvesttime," Amelia concluded her twin's sentence.

"But you have heard my stories so many times before, and your father has been there himself," Juliet said, smiling at each of them in turn. "He knows Louisiana is a beautiful place, although it is very different from England in its climate and way of life. Indeed, I grew impatient with the slow, unhurried pace at times."

"I believe you said you had lived there for some years, ma'am?" the duke asked.

"Yes. I was there almost nine years," Juliet replied.

"I do not think I would like to be away from home that long," Amelia remarked, her voice thoughtful.

"Nor I," Anne agreed. "Didn't you miss England, Juliet?"

"Very much, but I grew accustomed to it," Juliet told her, unaware that her voice had grown stiff and her eyes wary. The duke watched her carefully, his dark eyes hooded.

Juliet wiped her lips on her napkin then and placed it beside her dessert plate. "A delicious luncheon, your Grace, but I must be getting back to the manse now," she said. "Romeo will have the groom out to discover what has become of me if I stay longer."

The duke rose and came to help her from her seat, waving the hovering footman away. "Mind your train, ma'am," he said softly, and her hazel eyes flashed.

"I shall order your horse, m'lady," he went on more loudly. The twins opened their mouths in unison, but before they could speak, he added, "I shall, of course, accompany you."

Juliet looked up into his mocking eyes. "Please do not trouble yourself, sir. It is only a short distance."

The duke smiled. "But I am riding that way in any case, ma'am. There is a matter of business I must attend to in Barnstaple."

Juliet was glad when he turned away from her then, so he would not see the chagrin she was sure washed over her face. How neatly he had turned a compliment to her into a prosaic bit of ducal employment. William Fairhaven was too smooth, too quick, too sophisticated for her to feel any confidence in sparring with him. His whole attitude was complacent, as if he knew he would win any encounter between them. How much I dislike the man, Juliet thought.

"Would you care to ride with me, girls?" he was asking now. The twins were quick to agree, telling him it would take but a moment for them to change into their habits.

They excused themselves and hurried away, and Juliet walked to one of the windows of the morning room. There was no need to feel so breathless and trembly, she told herself. The footmen were still clearing the table, and she could hear the soft words of Devett as he directed them.

"Why is it I cannot rid myself of the feeling that you would do almost anything to avoid being alone with me?" the duke murmured from close behind her. He sounded amused.

"You are mistaken, your Grace," Juliet replied. "I do not intend any rudeness."

"But my wits have gone begging," he continued as if she had not spoken. "I have been most remiss not to remember this strange antipathy you have for men—any man. And that reminds me as well that I have yet to discover the reason for it." Juliet heard his soft chuckle, and she stiffened. "I shall discover it, you know. You may wager on it, m'lady," he told her.

His voice was determined and yet lightly amused, as if this was a small matter. Stung, Juliet said, "Why do you persist in this, sir? You know it is something I do not care to discuss, and yet you are so unkind as to continue to press me."

William Fairhaven put his hands on her arms then and turned her to face him. Juliet's heart began to pound at the warm strength of those fingers that seemed to burn right through her habit.

"But I am never kind, dear ma'am," he told her, holding her gaze. His mouth curved in a smile. "That is a characteristic of lesser men. And surely you would not deny me the solution to this little enigma."

"I do deny you," Juliet told him, proud of her cool voice and the way she was ignoring his nearness, that handsome face and sculptured mouth, those arching satanic brows over hypnotic dark eyes. "What I feel—what pleases or displeases me, is none of your concern. I am a very private person."

The duke inclined his head. "That is a hit, ma'am," he said as coolly as she had spoken. "And yet, I think I shall still accept the challenge. There is so little to do here at Severn, and so much time. Eventually I shall solve this mystery."

Remembering her imminent departure for London gave Juliet the courage to stand still in his grasp, even to smile a little. "We shall see, your Grace," she told him.

His eyes caressed her face and the little mole beside her mouth. Juliet was suddenly aware that the servants had left the room as the duke moved closer, his hands tightening on her arms as his dark head bent over her. "*En garde,* ma'am," he said. "I warn you that dukes, especially this one, always get what they want."

Juliet made herself laugh at him, and then she made an impatient motion. He let her go at once and she went gracefully to the sofa, where she had left her crop and riding gloves. Putting the little whip under her arm, she pulled on her gloves, saying as she did so, "Another salutory lesson is in order for you, I believe, sir. Even a duke cannot force me to disclose my thoughts. They are my own. Furthermore, I resent being used as a form of entertainment to keep you from being bored during your stay in the country. I consider you arrogant beyond belief and I shall not be a party to this charade. But you shall see."

The duke's bow was ironic and his expression disbelieving, but Juliet stood calmly, proud of the way she had held him at bay. She would begin her packing immediately, she told herself, and as soon as she had a reply from her aunt, she would be gone, and the Duke of Severn could whistle for her. He was not as omnipotent as he believed.

The twins rejoined them then, and the four went out to where their horses were waiting for them in the brilliant September sunlight.

The duke was a little abstracted on the ride to Barnstaple, a fact his daughters noticed with a great deal of satisfaction. He had bidden the Lady Juliet good-bye with his usual courteous aplomb, but Anne noted the little line that developed between his brows shortly thereafter, and Amelia, his silence and the tight set of his mouth.

William Fairhaven was indeed pondering the difficult and reluctant Lady Juliet. There had been something different about her today. She had seemed to have herself under better control, as if she held some advantage in their relationship that he knew nothing about. The only time she had reverted to her former, frightened behavior was when he had caught her up in his arms when she had almost fallen while dismounting. The way she had stiffened, her white face, why, it was almost as if a man's touch was not only unwelcome, but repugnant to her. But how could any woman with the lush figure of Juliet Manchester, those high round breasts, supple waist, and swelling hips, that soft smooth skin that was made for a man's lovemaking, be so perverse? Surely something had happened to her at one time to give her this dread of his sex, and he found himself more determined than ever to discover what it was. It was not just a way to pass the time and alleviate his boredom, as she had claimed, for in some strange way, she mattered to him.

Besides intriguing him, Lady Juliet attracted him, and he found himself wondering why. It was true that she was lovely, but she was not a beauty, and he always chose beauties as his flirts. Her face was merely charming, and there was nothing beyond her speaking hazel eyes and that bewitching beauty mark that was in any way outstanding. And yet, when she spoke or smiled, she seemed beautiful. Her figure was excellent, and her carriage and movements animated and graceful, and to add to her physical appeal, she was intelligent, well-read and -traveled. That was obvious from her conversation and wit. And it pleased him that she was not a silly young woman. It had been a long time since he had been attracted to girls in their first, or even their second or third Seasons, although he knew very well he would not have been interested in many of them at any age. There were so many foolish society women. And although silliness could be excused as a charming folly in youth, it was nowhere near as appealing at forty as it was at twenty.

But Lady Juliet was not silly. He doubted she ever had been. There was wisdom in her expression, and something else as well. Deep in her hazel eyes was a knowledge of human frailty and a calm acceptance of it that she met with a straight back and a head held high. She seemed to be saying by her attitude that although life might deal her any number of disappointments, she would shrug them away, in no way surprised by the vagaries of fate. And if she could not overcome these

131

problems, she would find some way to circumvent or live with them. She was a delightful, captivating puzzle, one that he was more than ever determined to unravel.

He saw her only twice in the next two weeks. She came to dinner one evening at Severn with her brother, but that could not be said to be a success from the duke's point of view, for they were constantly in the company of the others and there was no chance for any private speech. She had not ridden alone again, although he had looked for her, and when questioned, she said she was much too busy at the present time for such amusements.

And then, the Fairhavens received an invitation to tea at the manse. Romeo had insisted on it, for he said that they must repay the duke's kindness, and after a brief argument, Juliet agreed. She had heard from the Lady Elizabeth Pettibone, the Marchioness of Hanover, and knowing she was to leave for town in two days' time, gave her all the courage she needed. She had asked her brother to say nothing of her departure the evening they had gone to Severn, but now she knew she could not restrain him any longer. In a way, she was looking forward to observing the duke's reaction when he discovered that the woman he was playing with, the way a cat toys with a mouse, was soon to escape his grasp.

She did not have to wait very long, for when Anne asked her to come up to the hall to see the new dresses they were having made, she shook her head.

"How I wish I could, my dear," she said easily, "but that will be impossible. I leave for London on Thursday."

Out of the corner of her eye, she saw the duke put his teacup down on the table beside him. Over the twins' disappointed cries, he said, "So, you are leaving us, Lady Juliet. Now, what prompted this sudden decision, I wonder?"

Juliet smiled as she turned toward him, holding out a plate of queen cakes. "It was hardly sudden, your Grace. I have been planning to go for some time now."

The vicar beamed. "I am so glad that my sister has succumbed to the lure of town at last. And m'aunt Elizabeth will see to it that she has a fine time, I am sure. I do not not look for your return until Advent is well advanced, Juliet."

Before he could continue, Juliet interrupted. "I shall miss you very much, my dears," she told the twins, wondering why they looked so stricken. After all, they were happy with their father now. Why should her departure affect them so much, throwing them into such a fit of the dismals? Why, they almost looked as if they might break into tears.

"Perhaps you will not have to miss them, ma'am," the duke said, and her head swung around so she could watch him warily. "I myself have been thinking it might be a very good thing if I took the twins to London."

"To London?" Anne asked, almost spilling her tea in her excitement.

"Us?" Amelia chimed in, in an awestruck voice.

The duke crossed his long, tightly breeched legs and sat back at his ease. As it always was, his attire was faultless, from his glossy boots to his smooth-fitting coat of dark-blue superfine, and his spotless white linen. In his cravat, he wore an onyx stickpin, his only jewelry except for his huge gold signet ring. His smoothly brushed hair gleamed like black satin. Juliet saw his eyes intent on her face and tried to keep her expression neutral.

"Of course," he told the twins. "I most certainly do not feel able to leave you to your own devices yet, even with the new portrait installed to give you pause." As they looked uncomfortable, he added, "But that was unkind. To be truthful, I think it is time you saw something more of the world than Devon. Perhaps a good drawing master should be found for Amelia and a singing teacher for Anne. You have a lovely voice, my dear, but it needs training."

The girls hugged each other in their delight, and then he said, "Besides, there is the matter of a new governess as well. I could engage one myself, but I think we might have better success if you were to agree with my choice. That way she might be persuaded to remain for more than a fortnight."

"Oh, Father," the twins cried in that now-familiar reproving way, until they saw by the twinkle in his eye that he was teasing them.

Juliet felt as if she were stifling. He was not going to stay in the country; she would not escape him after all. And then she remembered how large London was. Surely she could avoid him more easily there than she had ever been able to do down here in Devon. The thought gave her the courage to smile at him.

"But how delightful, your Grace," she said evenly. "I am sure the girls will enjoy the jaunt and all the wonders of town."

"You *must* go about with us, Juliet," Anne begged. "It won't be nearly as much fun without you."

"Oh, do say you will see us as often as you do here at Severn," Amelia implored.

To Juliet's surprise, the duke intervened. "But you are being rude and thoughtless, m'ladies. You must not expect the Lady Juliet to curtail her own, mmm, excursions and amusements, to join you in yours. She will have other things to do in town, things much more interesting to her than the company of thirteen-year-olds."

The twins looked mutinous and so disappointed that Juliet hurried to say, "We shall see, m'ladies. Of course I will visit you sometimes. Your father is too harsh. Besides, I do enjoy your company. You are my good friends," she added, and both girls gave her a grateful smile.

As the trio was leaving the manse a little later, the duke found a moment to murmur to his hostess, "You did notice I did not ask if you enjoyed my company as well as my daughters, ma'am? I am not so brave—or so foolish."

Juliet gave him his hat and then she curtsied. "I am sure you were very wise to restrain yourself in this instance, your Grace," she told him with a triumphant smile.

"But, then, there are so many occasions that are not suitable for very young ladies, are there not?" he mused. "A ball, or a reception, for example. At thirteen they are years from being out; there can be no question of them accompanying me to any evening party. We are sure to meet there, Lady Juliet. How I look forward to it!"

Juliet's smile did not falter. In a crowded ballroom or formal reception she did not fear the duke. There was nothing he could do to her there but talk to her, and talking was something she could parry with ease, no matter what scandalous topics he introduced.

"I look forward to it as well, your Grace," she agreed, her voice so cordial it caused his slashing brows to soar. "I quite depend on you to introduce me to your friends. There can be nothing so lowering as attending a party where no one is known to you."

The duke's white grin surprised her. She had thought he might take umbrage at being used solely as an entrée to society, so arrogant as he was. "It is uplifting to know I am to be of some use to you, m'lady," he told her. "I shall strive to do my, mm, my humble best, but I cannot promise that you will be the belle of London as no doubt you were of Louisiana. That will be up to you."

Juliet did not let her smile fade as she walked with him to the door. They were followed by the twins, whose excited chatter to the vicar about the trip covered their conversation. "I have no desire to be a belle, sir. How absurd, at my age!" she said evenly.

The duke took up her hand and kissed it in farewell, and her composure slipped a little. He had never honored her this way before, and she found the touch of his warm lips on her skin and the pressure of his fingers upsetting.

"Pray restrain yourself, ma'am," he said as he released her hand at last. "You are not at your last prayers or quite an antidote yet. If you were, I can assure you I would not be seen with you."

The twins swirled around them then, cutting off any reply Juliet might have made to this outrageous statement, and in the flurry of leavetaking there was no time to say any more.

As Anne danced down the path, she turned and called back, "So Melia is going to leave home after all! I wonder if any of the other predictions the gypsy made will come true?"

Both girls laughed so heartily that the duke was forced to call them to order as he helped them into his phaeton.

Juliet wondered why she lingered in the doorway of the manse to wave to them as they drove away. Surely it was not for another glimpse of the Duke of Severn's exultant smile!

11

The city of London seemed vast and crowded and noisy after the peaceful English countryside and the drowsy southern plantation she had known. Juliet wondered if she would ever get used to it, for there were few hours of any day that could be considered conducive to quiet repose. She went to bed in her aunt's town house on Chesterfield Street with the sound of hansom cabs still rumbling by beneath her window, and as she closed her eyes, she could hear the occasional bursts of laughter and song as late-night revelers made their unsteady way home. And when she woke, more often than not, it was to tradesmen calling their wares, and the sounds of carts and barrows and the *clip-clop* of many horses as they clattered over the cobbles.

Of course she had visited the metropolis many times before she went to America, and she had stayed there with her aunt for some two weeks on her return before she went into Devon. The Marchioness of Hanover, the Lady Elizabeth Pettibone, was her mother's oldest sister. Relationships had never been cordial between the sisters, and so although Elizabeth had made a great marriage to a wealthy peer, it was not to her arms that Cecily Manchester had fled at the death of her husband.

If the truth were to be known, she had not been invited to do so. Lady Elizabeth made no secret of the fact that she did not feel any obligation whatsoever to house and pamper the widow. She knew Cecily had an ample jointure, and she said that if she had not been such a greedy namby-pamby, she would have made her own arrangements for herself and her daughter, instead of trying to hang on her older sister's sleeve.

In fairness to her, it must be explained that Lady

Elizabeth had offered Juliet a home, for she was fond of her niece. She had often remarked that while Juliet might have inherited her mother's looks, it was plain that her common sense and intelligence had to have come from the Manchester side of the family, since both her sisters had more hair than wit. Lady Elizabeth was known for her blunt speaking.

But at the time, still mourning her father and only just eighteen, Juliet had made no push to remain in England as her aunt's guest. Her mother was horrified at the very idea, claiming she could not possibly brave an ocean voyage or the travails awaiting her in a strange, primitive country without her daughter to support and sustain her. Juliet had resigned herself to it; indeed, she felt it was her duty to stand by her mother in her trials, never dreaming what such nobleness would cost them both.

Some years later, in 1813, Juliet had arrived at her aunt's town house little more than a week after the tea party with the Fairhavens. The journey had been made without incident, although it had been long and tiresome. Cooped up in a post chaise with only her maid to talk to, she had had plenty of time to think. Unfortunately, the Duke of Severn seemed to invade her mind more often than not.

Lady Elizabeth welcomed her niece warmly and insisted she come into the drawing room until her trunks and portmanteaus had been carried up to her room.

"Much better, my dear Juliet, to escape the hustle and bustle. Fanning will take care of everything," she said in her deep, booming voice as she waved to her very correct butler.

Her aunt motioned her to a chair and poured them both a brimming glass of sherry before she came to sit across from her niece. "That is a stunning hat, Juliet, but do remove it. You will be so much more comfortable."

Juliet recalled that her Aunt Elizabeth was famous for giving orders that she expected to be obeyed without question. She would not have put it past her to march up to King George to tell him how the war should be conducted, state affairs run, and the empire expanded.

"How nice it is to be here at last," Juliet said now as she removed the offending hat. "Thank you for inviting me, ma'am."

"Pooh!" Lady Elizabeth boomed, waving her wineglass. "You know very well I have been trying to get you to town ever since you returned from that impossible, rebellious former colony." She sniffed, not at the treason of the United States, but because she was still affronted that her earlier invitations had been refused.

Juliet smiled at her. The Lady Elizabeth was a very tall, slim woman in her sixties. Always elegantly gowned and coiffed, she was a leader of fashion. She had never been a beauty, for she had a long thin nose, a sharp chin, and slightly protuberant gray eyes. Her lack of beauty had never bothered her. She had often been heard to say she was glad she had inherited all the brains in the family, since she could never have endured going through life being the perfect widgeons her sisters were, although, as she was quick to point out, it certainly had never seemed to bother them.

Her brusque honesty was disliked by many, but since she had acquired the reputation of one of society's premier eccentrics, she was not only tolerated but lionized, and her blunt set-downs were repeated throughout the *ton* as the epitome of wit.

Her husband, the marquess, was a scholarly man who rarely left his estates in Surrey, so he was nowhere near as well-known as his wife. Juliet had often wondered at their marriage. They had no children and seemed perfectly content to live apart.

"You will want to do some shopping, my dear," Lady Elizabeth was saying now in her positive way. Not allowing her niece to comment, she went on, "Yes, yes, I know you have all the latest fashions from France, but your immurement in the country for nine months makes replenishment of your wardrobe a necessity. That is a very smart traveling outfit, by the way. I approve."

Juliet smoothed her beige twill gown with its dark-brown velvet trim and gold buttons, and nodded her thanks.

"And then there are several invitations that I have accepted for you," Lady Elizabeth went on. "You may be sure I have been busy informing the *ton* of your arrival, for we must make haste."

"Make haste?" Juliet asked, her voice wary.

"But of course. You are, by my calculations, thirty-one now, my good girl. A suitable *parti* must be found for you without delay. Thank heaven you have kept your figure, and although you are not a raving beauty, you have a pleasant face and manner. Your birth is excellent and your intelligence cannot be faulted. Furthermore, your portion is not in the least despicable. With so many attributes, I am sure we will have no difficulty at all, in spite of your age, but it must be done before another year passes. Should you object to a widower? Or perhaps someone a year or so younger than yourself? I have several candidates in mind."

"Aunt!" Juliet exclaimed, leaning forward in her earnestness. "I beg you not to disturb yourself on my account. I do not care to marry. In fact, I will go further and tell you I will refuse any offer, no matter how flattering."

"Why?" Lady Elizabeth demanded.

"Why?" Juliet repeated, at a loss to explain.

"Come, come, my dear, you are not an idiot, and so I believe you understand the qestion very well. Why *don't* you wish to marry?"

"I am too old for it, too set in my ways to change," Juliet said finally, trying to smile.

"Too old? You are little more than a girl," her aunt snorted.

"At one and thirty, ma'am?" Juliet asked.

"You must realize that anyone under forty is young to me, but that is enough of your roundaboutation, Juliet. What is the *real* reason?"

Juliet rose to pace the drawing room in some agitation, and her aunt watched her shrewdly. She could see the girl was upset by the way she clasped her hands together and set her lips, and she wondered at it as she sat waiting for her answer.

"I have discovered that I do not, er, care for men," Juliet said at last. She spoke over her shoulder, allowing her aunt to see only a part of her profile under her wealth of ash-blond hair.

"And what has that to say to anything, miss?" her aunt demanded, sounding as if she were puzzled. "I don't care for 'em myself, but that has nothing to do with marrying one of 'em. A spinster in this day and age is an oddity, a person of little consequence who is often held up to ridicule. Therefore, it behooves you to give up the single state and wed as soon as possible. And then, in a very short time, you will be able to go your own way, if that is what you wish. Husbands are not as demanding and time-consuming as you seem to think. A little resolution on your part is all that is needed, and the gentleman you honor with your hand will take his proper place in your life."

"What place is that?" Juliet could not help asking, intrigued in spite of herself at her aunt's unusual definition of marital bliss.

"Why, as the man who gives you the protection of his name and the use of his title, and who provides for you as lavishly as possible. He also serves as your escort on state occasions, although it is not at all necessary to keep him around, kicking his heels, at any other time," Lady Elizabeth explained, going to pour herself another glass of sherry.

"That does not seem very fair to the gentleman, Aunt," Juliet could not help observing, her voice quivering.

"Of course it is, and just what they deserve. You may explain the situation to your husband as soon as the ring is on your finger. He will soon adjust. Besides, men are not at all averse to setting up a mistress; indeed, they seem to feel it is expected of them. Idiots!" she scoffed. "They are like little boys, every one of 'em, trying to show that their manhood and virility are superior to that of their friends. They are muttonheads!"

She snorted again and tossed off her sherry. Juliet suddenly remembered her aunt's liking for spirits. She had often boasted she could outdrink any man of her acquaintance, and often had, although no one had ever seen her even slightly tipsy. Juliet's mother had claimed in a despairing voice that Elizabeth had a cast-iron stomach and a hard head, and it was too bad, for it was not at all ladylike. Needless to say, Lady Elizabeth had ignored all her admonitions and done just what she pleased.

Now she put her glass down on the table at her side and peered at her niece as a sudden thought occurred to her. "Pray do not tell me you are waiting to fall in love," she said, her voice rich with scorn. "Now *that* I could never abide."

"No, I do not want to fall in love," Juliet answered in even tones. "I do not want to marry at all. You must believe me, Aunt, for I am adamant."

The Lady Elizabeth looked as if she would very much like to continue to argue the point, but something in Juliet's hazel eyes deterred her. She realized there was more to her niece than she had imagined, and remembering how Juliet had insisted on burying herself in Devon in spite of all her entreaties against such a course made her cautious. The gel was stubborn and opinionated, but they would see who won this battle in the end.

"Come, my dear, I will take you up to your room so you might rest and change. We have been invited to a reception at Lady Booth's this evening, and I want you to look your best. Tell me, does that simple-looking maid you have with you have any skill at all? If she does not, our first order of business will be to engage a smart dresser."

As she spoke, Lady Elizabeth led the way to the hall, and she continued to chat as she accompanied her niece upstairs to her room. Juliet did not even try to explain that she was tired and would prefer to have her supper on a tray and an early bedtime. She would try to be amenable to her aunt's plans when she could, but in some things she would go her own way.

In the days that followed, she was very busy, caught up in all the activities that made up the Little Season. Sometimes she felt as if she never had a moment to herself, for her days were crowded with shopping and calls, and all manner of amusements. Her aunt introduced her to everyone who was anyone, but although Juliet met several ladies, she could see that her aunt's emphasis was placed firmly on the male of the species. Indeed, the lady often beguiled the drive home at the end of a party by listing the assets, complete lineage, and desirability of the gentlemen who had paid court to her niece.

Juliet did not bother to argue or protest, for she told herself that even Aunt Elizabeth could not force her to the altar against her will.

And then, one evening some two weeks after her arrival in town, she came off the dance floor of Lady Jersey's ballroom to find herself face to face with the Duke of Severn. He was standing beside her aunt, engaging her in light conversation, as tall and handsome and compelling as ever. Of course he would not forget the name, Juliet told herself bitterly even as she curtsied to her partner and gave him a warm smile in farewell.

"Servant, m'lady," the duke said, bowing as she came up to them. Lady Elizabeth looked from one to the other with great interest. My word, Severn! she thought. Why didn't I think of him?

"Although we just arrived today, I hurried to attend Lady Jersey's ball, for I was sure you would be anxious to know your friends have come," the duke told her. "The Ladies Anne and Amelia send you their love."

He paused and his dark eyes seemed to imply he had brought his as well. When she lifted her chin in defiance and stared at him, his lips twitched with amusement.

"How delightful, your Grace," she said, keeping her voice calm. "I see I do not have to make you known to my aunt, the Marchioness of Hanover?"

"We are old friends, are we not, ma'am?" the duke asked, bowing slightly to the older lady.

She laughed and nodded. "We are indeed, Severn," she said, and then she begged to be excused. "I see Lady Throckmorton waving to me, and I have the most delicious *on-dit* to tell her. I shall see you later, Juliet."

The duke and Juliet both heard the orchestra tuning their instruments for the next set, and calmly he took the little card that dangled from her kid-gloved wrist, to study it.

"But with the exception of this dance, you do not have a single one left," he said with admiration. "I see you did not need me to introduce you to society after all, Lady Juliet."

"My aunt has filled that role nobly, sir," Juliet told him, trying to keep the bitterness from her voice. Her aunt's pushing, authoritative ways had tried her patience more than once since her arrival.

The duke held out his hand. "Then I shall claim this

dance as mine," he said coolly. He listened as the first strains of music filled the crowded, brilliantly lighted room, and then he smiled. "How fortunate it is a waltz! You do waltz, do you not, ma'am?"

"Of course!" Juliet snapped, sure he was teasing her. It was obvious she was no debutante who needed the permission of the Almack's patronesses before she was allowed to engage in the German dance that was all the rage.

"I only asked because I was not sure the United States had allowed its importation," the duke said mildly. "They are so very strict, are they not? I have it on good authority that they consider the English nobility not only immoral but degenerate."

As he spoke, he led her to the floor and put his arm around her waist. Juliet stared at his dark evening coat as she was forced to put her left hand on his shoulder and surrender her right hand in his warm clasp. She tried not to think of his nearness, or how her skin was crawling under her pale-green satin gown with its overskirts of floating net panels caught up with pearl rosettes.

For a moment, they danced in silence, and then the duke looked down at her and said softly, "I am so glad you came to town, ma'am."

Juliet was forced to look at him, and her breath caught in her throat. He was too close, that handsome face bent over hers as if to possess her, while his dark eyes remained intent on her own. A tiny light gleamed in them, and she looked away in haste.

"Why should that be so, your Grace?" she asked, speaking to his right lapel.

"Because I would never have been able to dance with you in the country, and it is such a pleasure to hold you in my arms," he said in his deep drawl. "You are a warm, exciting armful, my lady Juliet. No wonder your dance card is filled."

Juliet refused to answer, and in a moment he said, "Are you angry that I followed you? But you must see it was no use to run away from me, ma'am. Dear me, I do seem to be afflicted with any number of females of all ages who think flight is the solution to all their problems. I wonder why?"

"Perhaps because flight is considered preferable to the company of the Dreadful Duke, your Grace?" she asked sweetly, feeling a stab of exultation that she had found a way to depress his pretensions.

His hand tightened at her waist and she could feel the muscles in his arm tighten as well as he drew her closer. It was all she could do not to cry out in protest.

"I believe the customary distance between the participants in the waltz is at least a foot, sir," she said next, hoping he did not hear the panic in her voice.

The duke did not move away from her. "Really?" he asked coolly. "But I have never concerned myself with what is 'customary.' "

Juliet felt the anger he was so easily able to make her feel begin to rise. "I forgot that you are the Duke of Severn and, as such, above all of society's strictures," she said. "One might even say a law unto yourself."

"But of course. Did you have any doubt of it?" he asked, and then he turned her in a sweeping curve as the music swelled. "How well you dance, my dear," he said.

Held locked against his chest, Juliet could feel his hard thighs brushing hers, and she began to tremble in earnest, feeling almost ill with distaste. The scent of his skin and the lotion he used seemed to be enveloping her in a warm fog and making her senses spin.

"Please," she begged in a little voice, "let me go."

"Look at me, if you please, m'lady," he ordered, and she raised her head, the sick misery of her eyes surprising him so much he almost missed his step.

He released the pressure of his hands at once,

although he did not let her go, and Juliet drew a deep breath, trying to suppress the waves of dizziness she felt.

"Why do you look that way? Are you ill?" he asked, nothing but concern in his voice now.

"I beg your pardon, your Grace," she whispered. "Yes, I am afraid I do not feel quite the thing. If we might sit down?"

The duke glanced around, and then he danced her quickly to the edge of the floor, avoiding the other couples with expertise. As soon as they reached it, he stepped back to offer her his arm. Juliet would have preferred to ignore it, but she knew she must continue the charade. He led her from the ballroom along the upper hall, which was thronged with guests, until they came to a small, empty salon.

"Sit down," he told her. "Will you be all right until I return?"

"I assure you I only require a little time to myself, your Grace. There is no need for you to return or—or concern yourself any further with me."

"Do try not to be so silly, ma'am," he said brusquely, and then he was gone.

Juliet leaned her head back on the brocade chair and closed her eyes. Her senses had not betrayed her this way in years. What was there about William Fairhaven that he could make her feel so strange? She had waltzed with other men who had held her close and whispered to her, and she had been able to dismiss their attentions with a shrug or a light laugh. But the Duke of Severn was another matter. When he was close to her, her heart pounded, her breath became shallow, and her skin grew cold with fright and apprehension. She must conquer this dread of him, for she could not allow him to have this power over her.

"What on earth?" she heard her aunt exclaim, and she opened her eyes to see her advancing into the salon, the plumes of her maroon turban waving in her agitation. She was followed by the duke, bearing a small glass of some amber liquid and a silver bowl and napkin.

"My dear Aunt, there was no need for you to interrupt your evening," Juliet began, but she was told brusquely to stop being such a pea goose.

"As if I would not come at once when I learned you were feeling ill," Lady Elizabeth said, her gray eyes protruding with her concern.

"Lean back, Lady Juliet," the duke ordered, dipping the napkin in the bowl he had placed on a nearby table. Juliet took a deep breath as he came closer, and then she did as she was bade and closed her eyes as well, so she would not have to see him. She felt a cold, damp cloth bathing her temples, and she sighed. After a few moments, she sat up and tried to smile normally.

"Thank you, your Grace. You are very good," she said, her voice wooden.

Lady Elizabeth stared at her. The duke did not seem to notice anything amiss however, for he went to fetch the glass he had brought. "Drink it," he ordered as he presented it. "It is only brandy."

Juliet pushed it away. "I cannot. It will make me feel even sicker, and truly I do not need it," she said. The duke did not insist, and when Lady Elizabeth saw how determined her niece was, she took the glass from him and dashed it down. "Can't let good brandy go to waste," she said. "And if you don't need it, Juliet, I do. Now, my good girl, what is this all about?"

Juliet looked from one to the other. The little mole beside her mouth seemed very dark in the pallor of her face. Seeing her hesitation, the duke bowed.

"Please excuse me, ladies," he said in his warm drawl. "I am sure Lady Juliet will be more comfortable in any of her confidences if I am not present. May I say how much I hope you feel more the thing soon, m'lady?"

He strolled to the door. Juliet could not take her eyes from his straight, broad-shouldered back, which tapered to narrow hips. And then he turned and said, "I shall do myself the honor of calling on you tomorrow, m'lady."

Before Juliet could deny him, he was gone, closing the door softly behind him.

Lady Elizabeth tried very hard to banish the self-satisfaction she was sure was written plain on her face when her niece turned to give her her attention at last.

12

True to his promise, the Duke of Severn arrived in Chesterfield Street late the following morning. He was preceded by a handsome nosegay of flowers that had been delivered early that morning. Juliet's maid brought it up to her on her breakfast tray, and the powerful, slashing strokes of his name on the card that accompanied it effectively destroyed all of Juliet's appetite for the scones, ham, shirred eggs, and piping hot coffee.

It was not her usual habit to breakfast in bed, but she had been ordered to do so this morning by her Aunt Elizabeth so she might regain her strength. Juliet could not refuse, especially since she had claimed that the reason she had felt faint the evening before was because she had been trotting too hard.

"You must remember I have led a very quiet life in the country, ma'am," she had told her aunt after the duke had left them. "I think this ceaseless activity I have been engaged in since my arrival in town has worn me to a thread."

After she had pushed her almost untouched tray aside, Juliet lay back on her pillows and, deep in thought, stared at the china ornaments on the mantelpiece with unseeing eyes. She was still disturbed by the way she had reacted to the duke's nearness and trying hard to discover some way to make sure it never happened again. She knew she could not avoid him. As long as he was interested in her, he would not permit it. But she had to wonder why he was? His attraction had been understandable in the country, for there were no other ladies around to amuse him, but surely now he was back in town, she could hope someone else, someone more yielding, who was not averse to a light flirtation or even a torrid affair, might catch his eye. And then I can be easy and comfortable again, she told herself stoutly, her hazel eyes darkening at the thought. I cannot bear this feeling I have to being controlled by him. It is exactly what I promised myself must never happen.

Because she knew, if she were to be honest with herself, it was not only revulsion the duke made her feel—oh, no, not at all. She was fascinated by him, drawn to him, always conscious of his powerful masculinity. Somehow he made her more aware of her femininity than she had ever been before. It was incomprehensible, because it was totally unlike her. It was almost as if he had put her under some spell. Even now, she was conscious of her naked body under the thin nightgown she wore and of the vague warm stirrings she felt just thinking about him.

At last she sighed and rang for her maid to help her dress. She had a luncheon party to attend with her aunt, and then a fitting on a new ball gown. And after that, tea at the Countess of Walmsley's, and a theater party to attend that evening.

After a bath, and dressed in a narrow gown of pale yellow, her heavy long hair done up in her customary chignon, and with a sarcenet stole draped over her arms, she came down to the drawing room with more assurance. Lady Elizabeth was entertaining two of her friends who had just called to show her the purchases they had made at the Burlington Arcade. Juliet joined them, delighted by the restraining presence of other company.

When the duke was announced, Juliet left the trio of ladies to go and greet him. His brows rose as he came in and found himself being observed by three pair of elderly eyes, and for a moment a little smile quirked the corner of his mouth. Juliet silently called herself to order.

"I do not have to ask if you have quite recovered, Lady Juliet," the duke drawled after making his bow to the other occupants of the drawing room. "You are in perfect looks, as always."

Juliet asked him to be seated, and then she thanked him for her flowers. Conversation did not flourish, perhaps because they were both conscious of the other ears that were probably straining to overhear them.

After a short silence, Juliet made herself say, "I am sorry you did not bring the twins, your Grace. I do so want my aunt to meet them."

"I had to be sure you were fully recovered before I brought those whirling dervishes, ma'am. I have come to agree with you that they are vivacious and charming, but when one is not feeling well, vivacious charm is the last thing one wants to have to deal with, especially when it is multiplied by two."

His drawl was sarcastic again, and Juliet made herself smile. "How do they like London, sir?" she asked next.

"The metropolis has received mixed reviews," he told her, an unholy light coming into his eyes. "Amelia seems impressed by the size and style of the buildings, but m'lady Anne says it is much too noisy and crowded, and that it, er, that it stinks."

Juliet's eyes began to dance, and she could not restrain a tiny gurgle of amusement.

"You may be sure I was quick to correct her, ma'am," the duke went on smoothly. "I told her it would be so much better if she would use another descriptive word. I even suggested 'malodorous,' 'fetid,' 'rank,' and 'offensive,' but all to no avail. She claims that no other word will do, for it most truly stinks."

Juliet was laughing out loud now, and the duke admired her animated face, the delighted curve of her mouth, and her sparkling, heavily lashed hazel eyes.

"Perhaps when she has had a chance to see the parks and some of the beautiful squares, she will change her mind, your Grace," she said. "And perhaps you could send her a posy of flowers to carry, so she will not be overcome by the, er, stench?"

They chatted then of the theater, and the balls Juliet had attended. Just before the duke rose to take his leave, he asked her to join them for a ride in the park the following afternoon. "We begin to interview governesses tomorrow morning, and I am sure we will be in desperate need of some diversion by then, m'lady. Say you will not fail us!"

Juliet told him she would be delighted and a time was set, and then she gave him her hand in parting. She was proud of herself that it did not tremble or grow damp as he held it in his and made his graceful farewells.

She was busy for the rest of the day, much too busy to think of the disturbing Duke of Severn, she told herself as she and her aunt were being driven to the theater where they were to meet the rest of Lady Elizabeth's party. But still she could not resist looking over the house from their box in the first tier, to see if he were present. To her surprise, she saw him enter a box almost directly opposite. On his arm was a beautiful woman. She had pale skin and eyes as dark as the duke's, and her black hair was dressed in an elaborate coiffure that

Well, the first one was nice and j[...] Anne told her.

But she was not at all acceptable t[...] [re]minded her. "She was much too, er, to[...]

"Why would that matter?" Juliet aske[d], [pu]zzled.

"She would never be able to keep up with the tw[ins,] [r]un after them when they were bent on mischief. Wha[t they] [r]equire, besides a woman of some learning, is a very [...] agile, quick-witted, *suspicious* type."

"Oh, Father," the twins exclaimed together.

"The next one was impossible as well. A Miss Prudence Augusta Kevington, if I remember correctly," the duke went on. "She was very prim and proper and earnest, and completely devoid of a sense of humor. The twins would drive her insane in a week. Perhaps in even two days' time," he added after a little thought.

"She was awful, Juliet," Amelia told her. "She never smiled once."

"And she had beady eyes," Anne agreed. "Just like a rat's."

"Before you insult the absent Miss Kevington further, shall we move on to the last candidate?" the duke intervened. "She was perhaps the best of the lot."

"No, Father, she was the worst," Anne corrected him.

"Why do you say so, Anne?" he asked as if he were genuinely interested. "Besides having a solid grounding in languages, mathematics, and history, she sounded as if she would be delighted to enter into all your pursuits, and she was all tender smiles."

"But it was because she smiled so much," Amelia explained. "Smiled and smiled and smiled! But not a [s]ingle one of them ever crinkled her eyes. They were [s]uch a cold gray. Brr! We didn't like her at all, did we, [A]nne?"

"No. She was the kind of person who would take

bared her slender neck and was secured by diamond combs. She was wearing a slim, revealing gown of scarlet satin, and her voluptuous breasts swelled above the low neckline. Juliet stared at her, wondering who she was as the lady smiled up at the duke and leaned close to him to whisper in his ear after he had seated her.

"That is Mrs. Kingley," Lady Elizabeth told her in an undertone. "She is one of Severn's old flirts. I thought their affair long since concluded; I am surprised."

"She is very lovely," Juliet made herself say, and then she pretended she had to rebutton one of her evening gloves so she could lower her eyes.

"And no better than she should be," Lady Elizabeth said tartly. Then she chuckled. "I might have known she would recapture Severn only a day after his return to town. The woman's like a man-eating tiger."

Juliet was reminded of the twins' assessment of the lady, and she looked across the theater again and had to smile. Yes, she did look sleek and pleased with herself, and hungry as well. Juliet's eyes went to the duke, to find him observing her through his quizzing glass, and she inclined her head, glad for some obscure reason that Mr. Ransom and Lord Wells, whom her aunt had asked to join their party, were such good-looking young men. The duke smiled at her and bowed in return.

Juliet saw that Mrs. Kingley was staring at her now, her expression haughty, and she tried to smile kindly at this perfect solution to her dilemma. Then she saw the lady's hand come up to caress the duke's arm as she melted against him again to whisper more secrets. They both laughed, and Juliet made herself turn aside and begin a lively conversation with her escorts.

The play that was presented that evening, although acclaimed as one of the Drury Lane's finest productions, seemed trite and flat and very unamusing. Juliet wondered that the others could exclaim over it so much.

* * *

When the Fairhavens arrived in Chesterfield Street the following afternoon, both Anne and Amelia were quick to dismount and run to greet Juliet when she came down the steps on their father's arm. They kissed and hugged her as if they had not seen her for months, and Juliet's embrace was warm and loving in return. The duke stood a little aside and watched her with his daughters, and he wondered why he felt the same little constriction in his throat that the twins were now able to call into being so readily.

Juliet allowed him to toss her into the saddle, and then the foursome began the walk to Hyde Park. The duke insisted Juliet take the lead with the twins behind her, while he brought up the rear. "I do not trust them on horseback in town as yet, m'lady," he explained while the girls looked affronted. When they had all passed through the park gates, he called them to a halt.

"No galloping, and no showing off, twins," he said sternly. "You will remember what I told you."

Anne's sigh was eloquent and Amelia's eyes begged Juliet for sympathy, but she only nodded her agreement. "Galloping is just not done, m'ladies," she said. "Your father is correct."

"Sometimes I think he is never wrong," Anne muttered, and the duke raised his crop in mock attack.

"Never," he said, his voice firm. "Keep it in mind. At all times. And now, shall we canter, ladies?"

It was a brisk afternoon, the sky full of scudding clouds that occasionally obscured the sun, and the park was nowhere near as crowded as Juliet had expected. When she saw the twins were on their best behavior, she began to relax and in a few moments found herself riding beside the duke, the girls following them. She had no idea how this had come about, for she wanted very much to talk to them.

Anne and Amelia exchanged a congratulatory glance

then fixed their bright-blue eyes [...] of them.

Juliet looks stunning, doesn't she, [...] [as]ked in a low voice. "That russet habit be [...]

"And it fits so well," Amelia said, admir[...] the material clung to Juliet's back and slim [...] wondered if she would ever have the figure J[...] and then she sighed. Even though she was begi[...] acquire breasts, they were very small, and Anne have any at all. The twins had fallen into the habit o[...] paring themselves in the pier glass after their baths Amelia was certainly winning the shape contest so fa[...]

After two complete circuits of the park, the d[...] slowed his horse to a walk, motioning the twins to do [...] as well, and then they all rode four abreast.

"You must tell me what you have been doing, m'ladies, and how you like London," Juliet said. Seeing the duke's warning glance to Anne, she added, "Aside from how it smells, of course!"

Both twins began to talk in turn, their voices animated, and their companions had little to do but smile and nod and exclaim. Finally, Amelia said, her voice a little subdued now, "This morning we [saw] several ladies who want to be our governess."

"I do not think I would go so far as to say [...] wanted to, especially after they met you, Amelia," duke corrected her in his slow drawl. "Surely [...] remember the lady who said she would have nothi[ng to] do with twins, for they were all imps of Satan. Sh[...] in a hurry, which was just as well, since I was ab[out to] agree with her."

The twins would have objected, but he we[...] smoothly, "And then, if you recall, we were all in[...] ment that none of the rest of them would suit."

"Why not?" Juliet asked, sure she was abo[ut to be] entertained in royal style.

great delight in pinching us or hitting us with a ruler," Anne said.

The duke seemed surprised at their perception, and he fell silent.

Then Juliet said consolingly, "But there are many governesses. Surely you will find someone you all will like."

"I hope we may, and in short order, ma'am," the duke drawled. "It is not my idea of the way to spend a pleasant morning, to be interviewing these ladies. There are so many other things I would prefer to do to occupy my time."

Juliet stiffened, remembering the luscious Mrs. Kingley. "Did you enjoy the play last evening, your Grace?" she asked, her voice carefully expressionless.

She did not see the twins glance her way at her change of tone, for she was intent on the duke's face. She thought she saw a warm, reminiscent smile there, and she wondered why she was so disappointed.

"It was excellent. Kean is a master, is he not?" the duke asked. "And that reminds me. There is a production of Shakespeare's *Julius Caesar* at Covent Garden I think the twins would enjoy. There is enough gore and intrigue to hold even their wandering interest. May we beg you to join us, m'lady, and for supper to follow?"

Immediately, the twins began to add their entreaties as well, and Juliet accepted.

"And you must come with us to the Royal Enclosure to see the wild beasts, Juliet," Anne said, and Amelia added, "And don't forget the paintings at the Royal Academy, and—"

"Steady there, you young hoydens," the duke admonished them. "Remember, Lady Juliet has her own amusements now. You cannot monopolize her time in town."

But in the days that followed, Juliet often found

herself in the Fairhavens' company. She invited the twins to tea so they might meet her aunt, but that could not be said to be a success. Lady Elizabeth said they were good gels and full of spirit, but she begged her niece to meet them somewhere else in the future. "I have never cared for the young," she said firmly. "They are so lively and precocious, they tire me considerably. Besides, they make me feel older than Methuselah."

Juliet laughed, but she was careful to keep the twins and her aunt apart from then on.

She went with them and the duke to the Royal Academy, and she chaperoned the girls on a shopping expedition to the Pantheon Bazaar. They were intrigued with the huge emporium, with more goods for sale than they had ever seen in one place, but after the stockings and the ribbons they needed had been purchased, they were quick to tell her they did not care for shopping as a whole. Besides, the duke had given them some money so they could treat her to ices at Gunter's, which they were sure she would enjoy a great deal more. It was obvious that the twins did.

The evening of the performance of *Julius Caesar,* Juliet dressed with a great deal of care. She wore her mother's pearl set and one of her prettiest gowns, a float of deep-gold silk trimmed with bands of creamy lace, and she allowed her maid to dress her hair in a softer style.

"You look very nice, Juliet," Anne told her, squeezing her hand as they took their seats in the box the duke had reserved.

"I like all those curls and waves," Amelia added.

"Father, don't you think Juliet looks lovely?" they asked together.

Juliet pretended to be arranging her stole. The duke had placed the twins between them, and now she looked up to see his admiring smile over their heads. "Very lovely, she always does. I wish both of you would try very hard to be like her. I am sure you would never find *her* sitting down to dinner with a smudge on her nose or a rip in her stockings.''

The twins sighed in unison, and Juliet had to smile at their put-upon expressions.

It was the first time the twins had been to the large Covent Garden, that famous theater that had been destroyed by fire in 1808 and then quickly rebuilt from a design by Sir Robert Smirke in 1809. They were fascinated by the noisy pit, the orange sellers calling their wares, and all the beaux ogling the painted ladies who paraded to and fro as if to show off their tawdry, colorful finery. In boxes like theirs, the gentry and members of the nobility sat in their jewels and satins and silks. Anne remarked that they were almost as noisy as the commoners below them, and Amelia said they seemed just as intent on showing themselves off.

But when the lights were dimmed and the play began, it was not long before the twins were leaning forward eagerly, their mouths a little ajar, as if they did not want to miss a single word. The crowded audience might well have disappeared for all they were aware of them.

When the assassination scene in the senate was being played and Brutus approached Caesar, Anne cried out, "Oh, 'ware Brutus!"

And then she blushed bright red as a gentleman in a neighboring box began to shush her. Juliet noticed the duke did not scold her or look black as he took her hand in his. She reached for Amelia's hand and was surprised at how tightly hers was gripped in return. When Brutus stabbed Caesar, both girls shuddered back in their seats, their eyes wide. Juliet wondered if it was not perhaps too powerful a performance for thirteen-year-olds, but at the play's end, after the farce had been seen and they were preparing to leave for supper, Anne exclaimed, her eyes luminous with satisfaction, "That was famous, Father! And so exciting!"

But there were other occasions when the twins were not present, just as the duke had predicted. Juliet met him at dances and breakfasts, at tea parties and musicales. He always came to her side, and he always asked her for a dance, but there was no repeat of what had happened during their first waltz. Juliet wondered if it was because she chatted in such a determined way about the twins. She noticed that, besides Mrs. Kingley, who was often present, the duke also honored a Lady Grandle, a delightful redhead who was much admired. Juliet told herself it was only a matter of time before the duke grew tired of their platonic relationship, and then she could be easy.

If Juliet was reassured that her problems were well on the way to being resolved, her Aunt Elizabeth was not so sanguine. She saw that the duke was not pursuing Juliet with any degree of fervor, for he seemed determined to cling to the single state he had enjoyed for so many years. Why, even the ladies he flirted with were all married and well aware of the rules of the game they were playing. It even occurred to her that William Fairhaven might only be using Juliet as a surrogate mother for his daughters, but she was careful not to mention this lowering thought to her niece. She did, however, turn her attention to other gentlemen of the *ton*. Perhaps Lord Quarls could be brought up to scratch? Or Mr. Wiley?

13

The duke, now that he had returned to town and all the amusements he ordinarily enjoyed, to the company of his friends and acquaintance, and the admiration of some very lovely ladies, would in all likelihood have relegated Juliet to the past tense as a "might have been" except for two very curious things. One was that she continued to intrigue him. He had yet to find out why she disliked men, and what had happened in her past to cause this antipathy, as he had promised himself he would do. And then there was the fact that the twins adored her. Since he was in their company so much, he could not fail to be aware of their very real affection for her. Sometimes he thought the Lady Juliet was all they seemed able to discuss.

He had engaged a governess at last, and he had great hopes that Miss Banks would remain longer than her predecessors. Anne and Amelia seemed to like her. She was in her thirties, and although she had all the learning the duke could wish for, there was a twinkle in her eye that told you she had a sense of humor that Anne and Amelia must admire as well.

With Miss Banks installed in his town house to chaperone the girls and take them about, the duke was free to go his own way. He was amazed to find he missed their outings, and he made it a special practice to take the twins to the theater or for a drive in the park as often as he could. He had also engaged a drawing master for Amelia and a singing teacher for her twin, and life in Berkeley Square settled into a pleasant pattern of lessons and practice that was carefully balanced by exercise and other amusements.

And then, at an evening reception, the duke asked the

Lady Juliet to drive in the park with him the following afternoon. He was denied.

"I am so sorry, your Grace," she said, her voice cool and even. "I have another engagement. Do tell the girls how sorry I am to miss the treat."

"They know nothing about it," the duke told her coldly. "I do not take them with me everywhere."

Juliet, who had seen him driving Lady Grandle only a few days before, nodded. She did not know if she were glad or sorry that she had promised to attend a loo party with her aunt.

The duke bowed and left her without another word, his expression noncommittal. The Lady Juliet did not seem to feel any warmer toward him than she had in the past, and this was something he seldom had to face. To say that it displeased him was to understate the case considerably. He spent the rest of the evening flirting with all the prettiest women in the room, and when he went home later, his pride was much soothed by their wholehearted admiration.

And then, one afternoon a few days later, he was reminded that he was also the father of three sons. He had left his room and was about to go downstairs when he heard his third son's voice coming from Amelia's room, and in astonishment, he paused to listen. Charles should be at Eton; what was he doing here in London?

"I won't tell you, Melia, so don't ask me," the boy said. The duke thought his voice sounded frightened and strained, and when it dropped an octave and then rose again in adolescent indecision, he was not tempted to smile. Instead, he edged closer.

"But you'll have to tell Father," Amelia pointed out. "Is it so very bad, Charlie?"

"Awful!" his son cried, and then there was silence for a moment. When he spoke again, there was determination in his boyish voice. "But I quite see it must be done, although I would rather talk to anybody but the Dreadful Duke about it.''

William Fairhaven's slashing brows rose. He had forgotten that terrible nickname.

"He is not dreadful at all, not anymore," Amelia defended him. "Why, Anne and I really love him."

Charlie snorted in disbelief, and she added, "I mean it! He is nowhere near as cold and stern and sarcastic as he used to be. But—but if what you have to tell him is very bad, Charlie, I must warn you that he has not completely reformed. You are sure to get a thundering scold."

"I know," her brother said, his voice despairing.

The duke went down the stairs then, deep in thought. When he reached the hall, he told his butler to have his horse returned to the mews, for he had decided not to ride that afternoon, after all. And then he went into his library and sat down to wait.

It was not very much longer before a timid knock came on the door, and he called, "Come in!"

As his son entered and bowed to him, he looked him over carefully. Charles was different from his brothers. Where they were robust and showed signs they were going to be as tall as their father, he had narrow shoulders like the twins, and a slender build with wavy dark hair and a pale complexion. Above a determined jaw, his dark-blue eyes were keen and full of intelligence. The duke thought he was a good-looking youngster, although at fourteen it was too early to tell what kind of man he might grow up to be. He realized he did not know his son very well and had no idea of his interests and dislikes. He only knew from the reports he received from the school that Charles Winston St. Marlystone Fairhaven, Viscount Hedding, was doing well in his studies, and showed an aptitude for crew and cricket as well.

"Good—good afternoon, sir," the boy said now, clenching his hands into fists to keep them from trembling.

The duke inclined his head and indicated he was to stand before the desk. "I am surprised to see you, Charles," he drawled, his tone mild. "There is some problem at Eton? A fire? An epidemic? Some other desperate reason for your arrival in town in the middle of the term?" the duke asked.

Charlie did not think he sounded very interested. He looked down at his feet and then back at his father. "Yes, sir," he said bravely. "There is a problem and I could not stay there. Not even for another day."

His voice cracked and a flush stained his cheekbones. The duke rose and came around the desk to pat him on the shoulder. To his surprise, Charles shied away from his reassuring hand. He looked white and frightened, and there were beads of perspiration on his forehead. The duke wondered why, but he only said, "It is a devil of a thing when your voice changes, is it not? Disregard it, my boy. We all went through it. It is part of becoming a man."

Charlie looked as if he could not believe that his austere, correct father had ever suffered such an agony, but he nodded, his expression a little brighter.

"And now I think you had better tell me what the problem is," the duke continued, leaning against his desk, his arms crossed over his chest. "Are you having trouble with your studies? Or perhaps some of the older, bigger boys are bullying you?"

Charlie looked affronted. "No, of course not. I know how to handle myself with bullies, sir, and my studies are going well. It is—it is . . ."

He stopped, an agonized expression on his face, and the duke waited. A number of possibilities ran through his mind. Had his son been caught gambling? Was he in debt? Surely it could not be a girl, not at his age. Or, horror of horrors, had he cheated on a paper or an examination?

At last Charlie said, "It's not the other boys, Father. It's one of the masters."

William Fairhaven's dark eyes grew keen under his hooded lids, and a wave of anger swept over him. He had not considered that possibility. "Indeed?" he asked, his drawl icy. "What do you mean, Charles? You will have to be more plain."

His son stared down at his scuffed boots again, and then he lifted that determined chin to look his father in the eye. The duke saw that the knuckles of his clenched fists were white with strain. "It's Mr. Frandom, sir. He's—he's cruel. He beats us."

"But masters have been thrashing students forever. I was often caned myself," the duke said at last, his voice even in his relief that the unspeakable possibility he had been contemplating was not true after all. "I have no doubt you deserve it sometimes, don't you?" he added.

"Yes, sometimes, sir. But it goes beyond a thrashing, and it's—it's not right," Charlie replied, sounding desperate.

The duke was pleased to see that he did not look away and his blue eyes were steady. And then, as if his admission had opened a sluice gate, the story poured out. Mr. Frandom had been beating him and some of the other boys ever since the summer term.

"He's my geometry master, Father, and he's in charge of my house. I could not avoid him," Charlie explained. "He seems to like beating us; he smiles all the time he's doing it. Sometimes he uses a cane and sometimes a leather belt. There's a boy in my form, a friend of mine, and he's not strong like I am. Why, after Mr. Frandom's last thrashing, Peter had trouble breathing for a long time, but he did not dare to go to the infirmary. I'm afraid he'll really be hurt next time. Mr. Frandom gets so worked up, it's like he's in a frenzy."

Charlie drew a deep breath, and then he said, "Yesterday he told me that if I dared to tell anyone about the beatings, he would hurt me even more."

The duke straightened and would have spoken, except Charlie went on in a rush, "So last night I slipped out after curfew and came up to town. I tried to think of someone else—anyone—I could tell. I was not sure you were not still abroad, you see. But even if you were not here, I had to leave and find someone to help us, all of us. I had to!"

His voice had risen, and it shook with fear and strain, and the duke in all his anger felt a real twinge of guilt. Charles had been trying to deal with this problem alone, since summer, and he was only fourteen. He had not known where his father was, and he had sounded as if he would rather speak to anyone else on earth but the man he should have been able to depend on.

Unable to speak for a moment, the duke went back around his desk and sat down to bury his face in his hands.

When he spoke again, his voice was calm and even. "Take off your shirt, Charles. I want to see what this Mr. Frandom has done to you."

Charlie seemed almost reluctant to do so, but at last he stood with his back to his father, his head bent. The duke could not restrain a gasp. The boy's back was covered with welts and half-healed scabs. Now he could see why he had moved away from his father's reassuring pat. The duke could not remember when he had felt such anger. Controlling himself, he said, "Yes, I see what you mean. This must be stopped, and stopped at once. Put your clothes on, Charles. In a little while I will put some salve on your back and you will feel better, but there is something we must do first."

As his son hurried to dress, he continued, "I want you to tell me the whole story, with as many details and dates as you can remember. And then tomorrow we shall both go down to Eton. I can assure you that Mr. Frandom will not be there for long. There is nothing he can do to you or any of the other boys again. I believe the Duke of Severn has enough influence in the world to ensure his immediate dismissal.''

His son's sudden beaming smile of relief made the duke's expression lighten a little. "Thank you, sir!" Charlie said eagerly. "That's famous! I'm sorry I had to bother you, but—"

"That will be quite enough!" the duke commanded, and Charlie's grin faded at his savage tone. "How dare you say it is a bother? How dare you imply your own father would not be concerned—" He stopped short then and waved a hand. "Sit down and start at the beginning," he ordered.

Charlie told his story, a little apprehensive at his father's cold, angry voice and rigid features. He was glad it was the geometry master who was going to be the recipient of his wrath, and not himself, and that when he had to confront the man, his father would be beside him. With the duke, he would not have to be afraid, for he was so tall, so powerful, so much in command. He was Severn, and to Charlie, he was invincible.

William Fairhaven put the guilt he felt at his son's ingenuous admission from his mind. He asked many questions and wrote down everything he was told. He would think about the problem of his relationship with his son later; at the moment, it was important that he get all the facts he could, so he could make sure that Mr. Frandom never again was allowed to deal with young boys.

They left the next morning, the duke's face still cold and set. He had not seen his children at dinner, for he had a previous engagement and he felt, in his anger, that that was just as well. Charlie had been warned to say nothing of the truth to his sisters, but to make up some story about debts.

When he was ordered to do this as they were leaving the library, Charlie grinned. He felt as if an enormous weight had been lifted from his shoulders, and already his back did not pain him so much. In his relief, he said airily, "But why not, sir? I don't understand."

His father's voice was calm. "They are young still and they need our protection from the ugliness in the world, now, and for some time to come."

When the duke returned to London some three days later, he was alone. Juliet had learned of Charlie's surprise visit from the twins and wondered at it, but she did not see the duke until a week had passed, and then only for a minute during an intermission of a concert they were both attending. Upon inquiring, she learned that Charlie had returned to school, and she wondered at the curt nod of satisfaction the duke gave, and his sarcastic, cutting voice as he said, "Where I am sure he will remain, and most happily too, until the Christmas recess. But I have begun to wonder how my family muddled through all these years without me around to solve their problems, ease their growing pains, and discipline them when they needed it." At Juliet's questioning look, he added, "You may be sure I shall be much more in evidence in the future, however much I deplore the necessity."

He changed the subject then, and a moment later Juliet's aunt came up and she had no further opportunity to discover what the young Fairhavens had been doing to upset their beleaguered father this time.

A week later, as Lady Anne dressed and got ready for breakfast, she suddenly realized that Amelia had not made an appearance that morning. It was very unlike her, and she frowned as she went down the hall to her sister's room.

She saw the maid had been in to make up the fire and

open the curtains, but Amelia was still in bed, her morning chocolate untasted on her nightstand. Anne could see at a glance that she was upset about something. And then, as she hurried up to the bed and saw the fright and horror in her twin's eyes, she cried out, "What is it, Melia? Why do you look that way?"

Amelia drew back from her outstretched arms and pulled up the sheet to cover her mouth. "No, Anne, don't come near me! Don't touch me! There is something wrong with me, something terribly wrong! I think I must be *dying*!"

The tears rolled down her cheeks and she sobbed, her blue eyes wide with horror and fright. Anne sat down on the bed and, unheeding, took her sister's hands in hers.

"Don't be so silly, Melia," she said. "No matter what it is, you know I will be with you."

Amelia still tried to push her away, but Anne was having none of it, and in a moment she had her arms around her sobbing sister.

"Tell me what is wrong, Melia," she commanded. "Why, it cannot be so bad, for you were fine just last night."

"That was at dinner," Melia sobbed. "But when I was getting ready for bed, Anne, I discovered I was bleeding to death!"

"Bleeding to death? Where?" her sister asked, her voice bewildered. Quickly she ran her eyes over as much of her cowering sister as she could see, but there was no sign of blood.

"Down there, between my legs," Melia whispered.

"Is it—is it a lot?" Anne asked, her voice awed now.

"No, but no matter what I do, I can't make it stop. Oh, Anne, I don't want to die! And I don't want you to catch it, whatever it is!"

"You mean it might be something like the Black Death?" Anne asked in a horrified voice. As Amelia nodded, she cried, "Oh, I wish we had never come to

London! It is so dirty and smelly! You probably caught it right here in town.''

"And now you will get it too," Amelia mourned.

Her sister squeezed her hand. "At least we'll be together, Melia," she said bravely, wondering if even now the plague germs were coursing through her body. In horror she wondered where *she* would start to bleed, but then Amelia cried even harder and she forced herself to put it from her mind.

"We must tell Father at once," she said. "Maybe there is something he can do, some doctor somewhere—"

"No, no, we must not go anywhere near him. He is Severn, and besides, I could not bear it if he were to die too, and all because of me. Promise me you won't tell him—or anyone!" Amelia demanded.

"Very well," Anne said slowly, and then she asked. "Does it hurt?"

Amelia shook her head. "No, that is what is so strange. There is only a little ache, not even as bad as a stomachache. But maybe it gets worse later."

Wet, despairing eyes looked into identical terrified ones, and the girls collapsed in each other's arms.

For a long time there was nothing but their sobs to be heard, and then Anne sat up and wiped her eyes, saying with great resolution, "We must go away at once, before we spread the disease."

"But where can we go?" Amelia asked, sitting up in turn and brushing her tangled black hair away from her face.

"We must leave London and go far away where no one knows us," Anne told her.

"How are we to do that?" Amelia asked.

"Can you ride, do you think, Melia?" Anne asked. At her sister's nod, she said, "I will order a horse brought around as if I were going for a ride in the park.

Then, somehow, I will lose the groom and meet you. And then we will make our way out of town and get away."

"Where will we go?" Amelia asked, trying to be practical.

"Why—why, we can go to Bath and drink the waters. They are very beneficial, I am told," Anne said hopefully. "Why, they might even cure us!"

"But we are only thirteen, and we have no money, and how can we take our clothes, or . . ."

Anne rose, looking determined. "We will have to find a way. We can pack a few things in the saddlebags. You'll have to carry those when you leave the house. As for money, I know where Father keeps his strongbox. We'll have to take some from there."

"Anne! That's stealing!" her twin said, her face white with shock at the very idea.

"I know it is, but we can't go off with nothing. That would really get us in trouble. And I'm sure Father would want us to take it, to protect ourselves. You remember what he said . . ."

"We must leave him a note, to explain," Amelia said.

Anne nodded. "Yes, for then he won't worry. What a good thing it is that Miss Banks has gone to visit her mother for the day!"

Amelia did not look as if she thought there was anything good in the entire world as the two put their heads together to devise a letter to their father.

"Perhaps we should tell Juliet," Anne suggested. "She might help."

"We can't do that, for then she will get the plague, too. No, we will have to send her a note as well," Amelia said, her lips set.

And then she added, "I am so sorry you hugged me, Anne, and caught it too, but I do not think I could bear to die without you!"

This called for more tears, and it was over an hour later before their notes were written and final preparations made.

Everything went just as they had planned. Anne dressed in a warm habit and bonnet and asked the butler to have a horse brought around. She explained that her sister was busy doing some extra work Miss Banks had left her, so she would be riding alone. Devett smiled and nodded.

Anne thanked him, stifling the remorse she felt for her lies, and then she went into the library, supposedly to wait for her mount and the groom. Instead, as soon as she had closed the door, she hurried up to her father's desk. The strongbox was kept in the deep bottom drawer that was always locked. She knew the duke kept the key with him, so she used his letter opener to pry the lock, trying very hard not to scratch the polished mahogany as she did so. It seemed to take an age before the lock gave, and she could not help looking nervously at the big double doors for the amount of noise she was making. The strongbox was not locked, for which she was grateful, although somewhat surprised. It seemed very careless, but perhaps Father felt that locking the drawer was sufficient.

When she lifted the lid, she could not help sighing with relief. There were golden guineas there, and smaller coins, as well as a fat roll of soft, and she scooped everything up. Wrapping it securely in her handkerchief so it would not jingle as she walked, she put it in her pocket. The weight made it seem like a lot. Surely there was enough so they could live in comfort until *the end,* she thought, willing herself not to cry again.

When Devett came in to announce that her horse was at the door, she was sitting in a large wing chair, riffling through one of the journals, the very picture of innocence.

She had left her father's note on the desk, and now she handed Juliet's note to the butler. "I amost forgot," she said brightly, trying not to breathe on him. "Would you be a dear and see that Lady Juliet gets this note, Devett? There is no hurry—late this afternoon will be plenty of time."

She smiled again and sauntered through the doors as the butler bowed. Outdoors, she was glad to see the groom in attendance was Albert Williams. He was getting old, and she knew he hated to gallop, which was why the duke left him in London all year. She waved him away and used the mounting block so he would not get contaminated, and then she turned her horse's head toward Hyde Park, the groom following a respectful distance behind.

She managed to lose him by suddenly galloping halfway through the park. As soon as she was around the next bend, she left the bridle path and cut across the carriageway into the park itself. As she rode around the Serpentine, she was glad it was still so early that few of the *haut ton* were in evidence. She did not care how many nursemaids and footmen walking m'lady's pugs pointed at her and exclaimed, as long as she made good her escape.

Once through the Stanhope Gate, she slowed her pace to a decorous walk as she made her way to the alley off Adams Mews, where she and Amelia had made arrangements to meet.

14

When William Fairhaven returned to his town house in Berkeley Square a little after one that afternoon, he found it in an uproar. His knock had gone unanswered for such a long time that he had finally opened the door himself, to stride into a hall that seemed filled with people, all of them talking at once.

He stood looking at them in amazement, and then Devett caught sight of him and hurried forward, his lined old face concerned. One by one, the others fell silent.

"I am sure there is some very good explanation for this unseemly noise and confusion," the duke remarked in his sarcastic drawl. "No doubt you will tell me what it is in your own good time. Do not feel you must hurry; I am at your disposal."

"Oh, your Grace," the butler said, his voice quavering, "it's m'ladies. They are gone again—disappeared!"

The duke handed him his hat, gloves, and clouded cane. His dark eyes raked the company, and his slashing brows drew together in a frown. The housekeeper was there, two of the upstairs maids, three footmen, the bootboy, and somewhat surprisingly, his elderly groom.

This last man shuffled his booted feet on the shining tiled floor and twisted his cap in his hands. "Run off from me in the park, that Lady Anne did, your Grace," he grumbled, looking affronted at such unusual behavior. "Just galloped away without so much as a by-your-leave, she did!"

"And the Lady Amelia is gone, too," Mrs. Pomfret announced, and one of the housemaids threw her apron up to her face and began to sob noisily.

"All of you will be silent," the duke ordered. He did not raise his voice, but its icy authority caused the maid to stop in midsob. As she gulped and wiped her eyes, the duke said, "Devett, tell me what you know of this, at once."

"Certainly, your Grace. I was waiting for a chance to do so," the butler said with dignity, glaring at his underlings. "Lady Anne asked for a horse this morning. She told me Lady Amelia was doing some extra school-work for Miss Banks, so she would ride alone. I sent to the stables, and Albert Williams brought the chestnut mare around."

" 'E knows I was there. Didn't I just tell 'im so, man?" the groom interrupted, and then he added in a chatty way, "I wuz ridin' the bay, your Grace." At the duke's angry glare, he colored up and fell silent again.

"And none of you saw the Lady Amelia?" the duke asked, looking at each one in turn.

The littlest upstairs maid opened her mouth, but no sounds emerged. The duke stared at her and she looked as if she were about to faint.

"Well?" he asked, and the housekeeper poked the girl, hard.

"I saw 'er, your Grace," she whispered, bobbing a curtsy. "I brought in 'er chocolate at seven this morning."

"Was she in bed at the time?" the duke asked, trying to make his voice kinder. He could see the girl was almost frozen with fear.

"Yes, sir, that she wuz, sir," came the whispered reply.

"Did you see her at any other time this morning?" the duke asked next.

"Oh, no, sir," the maid said, bobbing again.

"The young leddies dress themselves, your Grace," the other, older maid joined in eagerly. "They ring when they go down to breakfast so we'll know when we can do up their rooms." She paused for a pregnant moment, as if to prolong the suspense, and then she added darkly, "They did not ring this morning, sir. And some of their clothes is—is *missin'*."

The duke was forcibly reminded of his dramatic daughter Anne, and at his sudden dark frown, the older maid shrank back, looking as frightened as her coworker.

Devett sniffed. "Neither young lady came to the breakfast room, your Grace. I thought Lady Anne meant to eat after her ride in the park."

"What time did she leave the house?" the duke asked next.

"About nine-thirty, your Grace," Devett told him.

"Now, Williams," the duke said, turning to his groom, "there is only one horse gone from the stable?" At his nod, he said, "Tell me exactly what happened in the park."

The groom shuffled again. "We wuz 'alfway 'round Rotten Row when all of a sudden, she galloped away. I went after 'er, sir, but she just disappeared. I went all 'round the park twice, but there wasn't a sign of 'er. *And* she 'asn't come 'ome, neither, so it wuzn't a trick she was playin' on me, like *some* 'ere I could mention 'as claimed."

He looked darkly at the butler and one of the footmen, and then the knocker sounded a rapid tattoo.

The duke nodded to his butler, who hurried forward to open the door. The Lady Juliet Manchester stood there, looking somewhat less than her usual immaculate self. She was clutching a letter in her hand, and her eyes widened when she saw William Fairhaven and the assembled servants.

"Thank heaven you are here, your Grace," she exclaimed, moving toward him, holding out her hands.

The duke took them and bowed slightly, the pressure of his fingers requesting her silence.

"I take it you have heard from my tiresome brats, ma'am?" he asked easily as he tucked her hand in his arm. "Let us adjourn to the library. I am anxious to hear what you have learned." At the door he said over his shoulder, "That will be all. May I suggest you return to your duties? It is obvious that not a one of you know anything about where the twins can be found at the moment, and there is little that can be accomplished by your remaining here, milling about and speculating among yourselves."

As he closed the library doors firmly behind them, Lady Juliet said, "Yes, I have had a letter from the girls, your Grace, but I do not understand a word of it."

William Fairhaven was walking quickly to his desk, for he had spotted the square of white paper lying there. "That is hardly surprising, m'lady," he said. "The twins' spelling is atrocious. Aha, as I thought. I have a letter, too. Would you excuse me?"

Without waiting for permission, he ripped it open, and Lady Juliet went to sit on the edge of one of the velvet wing chairs, her eyes apprehensive.

She watched the duke intently as he read, and she could see that he was puzzled.

"What did they say?" she asked as he crushed the letter in his hand and stared at her as if he did not even see her.

"Here, read it for yourself. Perhaps you can discover what it means, for I assure you I cannot!" he snapped, tossing the paper to her.

Juliet smoothed out the sheet with shaking fingers. She read:

Dear Father,

We have gone away. But only becuz we *had* to. Truely we never wanted to run away again but something has happened. Something very *cerious*. We beg you to understand. It is for your sake, and Severn's, believe us. We had to take all the money from your strongbox in the liberry. Do not worry about us. We will be together at the end. We love you.

Your affecshunate daughters,
Anne and Amelia

There was a postcript: "Do not try and find us. We would not put you in *danger*!!!!!!!!"

Juliet gasped, and the duke said, "That was written by Lady Anne, I would wager any amount on it. And when I get my hands on that young lady, the first thing she will learn is that I will not tolerate her amateur theatricals a moment longer. What 'danger'? 'Together at the end'? The end of *what*?"

"My letter is very similar, your Grace," Juliet said, holding it out to him.

The duke took it and read it quickly. "The spelling does not improve, does it?" he asked absently. " 'Sir-uptishushly'? Good Lord!"

Juliet was rereading his letter. "Did you keep much money in the strongbox, your Grace?" she asked.

The duke went around his desk. His frown deepened until those slashing brows were a solid line across his forehead when he saw the scratches on the polished wood. He lifted out the box and opened it.

"I kept some four hundred pounds here for emergencies. It is gone, every last shilling of it."

"Then that means they are planning to be away for some time," Juliet said.

"But why?" the duke asked, sounding almost bewildered. "They have been happy lately—at least they appeared to be. And I could have sworn, after my last trimming, that such pranks as running away were a thing of the past."

"I do not understand it either, sir," Lady Juliet said, looking worried. "But somehow I do not think this is a prank. They sound too frightened, almost as if they were in a panic. This is more than dramatics, and I admit I am frightened. Where can they be? Where can we even begin to look for them in this vast city?"

"Thank you, m'lady," the duke said, going quickly to the door. "You have reminded me of what should have been my first order."

He opened the door and called to his butler, "Send the footmen running to each of the post roads going out of town in every direction, Devett. They are to see if they can find any trace of the Ladies Anne and Amelia."

He closed the door on the butler's quick assent, and as he came back, he said, "I do not think they are still in London, for if they planned to remain, why did they set up that elaborate ruse to get the horse? She would only be a burden here. No, they must have left town, and fortunately for us, they have a serious handicap, ma'am."

He looked more cheerful as he went and poured them both a glass of Canary. As he presented it to her, he said, "They are identical twins. Who could fail to remark them, dressed alike and both riding a thorough-bred horse? We will discover the route they took in short order. In the meantime, there is nothing we can do but wait. Do drink your wine. I pride myself on my cellar, and I can assure you the Canary is excellent. Besides, you look as if you need it, and you must keep up your strength. You see, once again I must command your assistance."

"Of course," Juliet said absently, obediently sipping her wine. She sighed and put it down on the table near her. "If only there was something I could think of, some reason . . ."

Her voice died away, and then she said slowly, "I saw the girls only two days ago. They were just the same as they have always been; I did not detect any shadows in their eyes and there was no hesitation in the way they spoke to me of their future plans. Why, Amelia was full of a boat trip down the Thames you had promised to take them on."

The duke leaned against his desk, crossing his shining boots. "That is true," he said. "We were to go in two days' time. They were anxious to see Eton, and I wanted to make sure Charles was all right. But since that was the case, what could have happened in the meantime that would cause them to write such letters as we have received?"

He shook his head, and then he said, his drawl noticeably absent, "I will never understand them, never! But when I recover them this time, their punishment will be swift and sure. I will not tolerate these catastrophes any longer. They will both be whipped and then I will have them watched night and day. And heaven help them if they ever, *ever* disobey me again!"

Juliet did not comment at the harsh program he proposed, but she knew she must be with the duke when he caught up with his daughters if only to curb the retaliation he planned now, in the white heat of his rage.

"If I might write a note to my aunt, sir?" she asked, rising and waving toward the desk. "I must tell her a little of the situation so she will not be alarmed at my absence."

The duke nodded. "I do not know if we will find them today, Lady Juliet. They have several hours' head start. I hope Lady Elizabeth will be able to accept it with a good grace if you must be away overnight."

Juliet looked up from her note, her color a little heightened. "I shall ask her to have a maid pack me a grip for overnight, sir. She is not a foolish woman and I am not a debutante; there can be no question of the proprieties at such an anxious time. Besides," she added almost absently, her eyes going to her note again, "in my case, the very idea is an absurdity."

The duke stared at her, bewildered not only by her words, but by the bitterness in her voice.

"If such a situation does arise, I shall say you are my sister, ma'am," he said, his drawl very noticeable now. "Although I doubt anyone would believe that such a blackbird as I am could call myself kin to a lovely golden canary."

"How fortunate that ladies are known to dye their hair, your Grace," Juliet said evenly as she sealed her note and rose to give it to him.

As he handed it to Devett to have it delivered, the duke pondered this strange acceptance of what might well turn out to be an embarrassing situation. But then he realized that the Lady Juliet was concerned for his daughters, as concerned as he himself, and because of this, she would ignore all of society's rules. It warmed his heart to know that she would be with him, that he did not have to face what lay ahead alone.

It was almost an hour later before the news was brought by a panting footman that the ladies Anne and Amelia had been seen on the road leading west out of London. The duke had ordered the carriage made ready some time ago and his portmanteau packed. Juliet's bag had been brought from Chesterfield Street as well.

Now he helped her to a seat, telling the coachman to spring the horses as soon as the outskirt villages had been reached. With them came two grooms, one on horseback and one sharing the perch with the driver.

Juliet stared at the busy streets they were passing through so slowly. In her head she kept repeating, Hurry, hurry! She knew she was as taut as a coiled spring, but she realized it had nothing to do with the duke's disturbing proximity. It was the twins. She wanted to reach them and help them as soon as it was humanly possible to do so.

The duke must have been under the same tension, for outside of a few, commonplace remarks, he did not speak. Certainly there was no repeat of his earlier love-making when they had been cooped up together chasing the girls when they had run off to the gypsies. Instinctively, this time, they both seemed to know that this was much more serious, much more than just another madcap prank.

When they reached Maidenhead, they had to stop, for there were two roads the twins might have taken. One led to Marlow and Wallingford, the other in the direction of Reading. The duke ordered the coachman to pull in at the best inn, and while the grooms went about asking questions, he engaged a private parlor and had the team changed.

To Juliet the wait seemed to take an age. She paced up and down the parlor, praying, and every so often she would go to the small window that overlooked the yard to see if any news had been brought.

At last, the duke came to fetch her. As he led her down the steep inn stairs, he said quietly, "They were seen on the Reading Road early this afternoon. The farmer's wife who spotted them described the horse and its riders exactly; there can be no doubt it was the twins."

The afternoon seemed to race by after that. Every so often, the duke would stop briefly at a village or crossroads, and he seemed reassured by the occasional report that the twins were still on this road, ahead of them.

They had almost reached Thatcham when he said, "I cannot for the life of me understand why they came this way. There is nothing ahead but the North Wessex Downs, and of course, Bath."

"It is a mystery," Juliet agreed. "But no doubt they had some very good reason, or so they thought."

The duke's black expression showed his disgust, and then the carriage swept into the village, and he banged on the roof for the coachman to stop. There were a few men outside an ale shop, and he called to one of them. Juliet was relieved when they discovered that the twins had been there only a short time before. The local told them they were leading a tired horse, and they had not tarried, marching through the village at a fast pace.

The duke rewarded the man with a few coins and ordered his men to keep a sharp lookout ahead, before he settled back on the squabs and said, "And now, my dear Lady Juliet, I believe we are about to catch up with them at last. If you have any desire to beg me to be merciful to the twins, you had better start pleading their case now."

Juliet smiled. "I only ask you delay their punishment until you learn why they ran away, your Grace. There must be a reason, even though we cannot fathom it at the present time."

The duke nodded and they fell silent, both trying to peer ahead through the limited view of the road the side windows provided. And then, just as before, the coachman bellowed for the team to halt, and Juliet braced herself with the straps as the carriage came to a stop by the side of the road.

The duke jumped down and extended his hand, never taking his eyes from his daughters. They were standing in a field that bordered the road, talking to an old farmer who was holding two broken-down hacks by their bridles. When they saw the duke and Juliet, they backed away, covering their mouths with their hands.

"Stay exactly where you are, m'ladies," the duke ordered in a harsh voice as he covered the ground between them rapidly.

The twins exchanged despairing glances, and then Anne called, "Stay back, Father! You must not come near us!"

"We're sick—*dying*!" Amelia added, her voice breaking.

"Now, what is all this nonsense?" the duke asked, reaching their sides and glaring at them. "You do not look as if you were dying to me. And if saying that is just to make me more lenient with you, understand that the ploy has failed. There will be no lenience this time, my girls!''

"No, no, keep away!'' Anne begged through her handkerchief.

"Juliet, do not let Father touch us,'' Amelia cried. "We are contimated.''

"*Contaminated*?'' Juliet asked, completely confused. "Whatever do you mean?''

"Amelia got ill last night,'' Anne explained. "And then this morning, I hugged her, so now I have the plague, too.''

The old farmer gave a high-pitched whinny. He had been listening avidly to this incomprehensible conversation, but since he did not think very highly of the gentry's good sense, the girls' statements only caused him to slap his knee with his hat and stamp his foot in merriment.

"Ee gorm, wot a tale!'' he crowed. '' 'Aven't laughed so 'ard since Farmer Petson's pig got loose and chased the vicar clear through the village!''

The duke ignored him. He had not taken his eyes from his daughters. He saw the fear in their eyes, but somehow he did not think it was a fear of punishment. They seemed terrified, as if they really did believe they had the plague.

"Why do you think you are sick?'' he asked, trying for a normal voice.

The twins looked at each other, and then they looked from the duke to the old farmer and the interested coachman and grooms who were all straining to hear. The farmer had even leaned forward and cupped his ear.

"We—we can't tell you,'' Amelia began.

"Not in front of all these people,'' Anne finished.

Juliet stepped forward then. "If I may, your Grace?'' she asked, smiling at her young friends. "Can you tell me, m'ladies?''

Anne and Amelia nodded, and she gestured to an old apple tree a little distance away. The girls walked toward it, still covering their mouths. The old farmer gave his high-pitched whinny again.

The girls would not let Juliet approach them too closely, but the duke could see her questioning them at some length and see the girls' answering as well. In only a few moments, she moved foward, shaking her head as she put her arms around them both and hugged them close. And then she began to talk to them. The duke noticed that neither girl took her eyes from her face as she spoke at some length. At one point, he heard Anne cry, "We're all right? Truly?" And a little later, Amelia's heartfelt question, "You mean I am not going to die? Cross your heart, Juliet?"

And then a terrible suspicion went through the duke's quick mind. No, it could not be! Surely someone must have told them before now, he thought wildly. And then he remembered his long-dead wife, the proper Mrs. Pomfret, and the steady stream of ever-changing governesses, and he shook his head at his folly.

The old farmer nodded in sympathy. "Know 'ow you feel, sir," he said. "Them gels 'ave been trying to swop that there 'orse for my two old nags this past 'our. I thought they stole 'er, and I don't 'old with stealin'. But I knew summat wuz amiss. Weren't born yestiddy, y'know. By the by, name's Elijah Jenkins. Lived 'ere all m' life, all fourscore years and two."

He beamed with pride, and then he added, "Them there leddies, as ye called 'em, well, I can tell ye, sir, they be a rare 'andful, ee gorm, yus."

"It is unnecessary for you to point that out to me, Mr. Jenkins, for as their father I am all too well aware of it," the duke said through gritted teeth.

He saw Lady Juliet coming toward him then, her face carefully expressionless. The twins dawdled along behind her, hanging their heads as she beckoned him to join her a little part from the others.

When he reached her side, he saw the little embarrassment in her eyes and the way she hesitated, as if she did not know how to put what she had discovered into words, and he nodded to her. "Can it be possible that my daughters have started their menses, Lady Juliet?" he asked, his drawling voice matter-of-fact.

Juliet nodded. "Amelia has. Last night she thought she was slowly bleeding to death, your Grace. She had no idea of what was happening to her and she was sure she had caught a horrible disease, perhaps even the Black Death. She tried to keep Anne away from her, but that Anne would not allow. And then, although they were frightened, they decided they had to leave London. They did it to protect you. Amelia said she knew she could not bear it if you died because of her."

The duke's expression did not change, but she saw the way his mouth tightened for a moment.

"Once again I am in error," he said, his voice strained. "What a terrible father I am! I should have made sure some woman told them of this long ago, so they could have escaped this needless day of terror."

"It was unfortunate, that is true," Juliet agreed. "But I have told them everything, and they are so glad they are not dying, I do not think it will have any lasting effect. They are young and resilient, your Grace."

He looked past her then, to where his daugthers were holding hands and whispering together.

"Where were they going?" he asked, curious now.

He was surprised to hear Lady Juliet's little chuckle, and when he looked at her, he saw her hazel eyes were dancing as she tried to restrain a heartier laugh. "To Bath, sir," she said, her voice shaking. "To, er, drink the waters."

The duke did not dare look into her merry face for a

moment longer, lest he disgrace himself. Instead, he turned away and called, "It is all right, twins. Get in the coach now."

The old farmer decided to reinforce the duke's command. " 'Ere, you young varmints, get in that there coach! You 'eard your da, didn't ye?" He shook his white head and glared at them. "Ought t'be ashamed o' yourselves, that's wot I say! Ee gorm, *females*!"

"Amen, Mr. Jenkins," the duke agreed, slipping a guinea into his hand. This unexpected largess silenced the old farmer at once, and even when the coach was driving away, they could see him turning it over and over and holding it up to the late-afternoon light to admire the shiny gold.

The mare was tied behind the carriage, and the duke gave orders to head for Reading. "It is late and we are all tired. Tomorrow will be time enough to return to London. A hearty dinner and a good night's sleep are what we all need, including the mare." He smiled at the twins, and when they would not meet his eye, he added gently, "There is nothing to be embarrassed about, twins. I am only sorry I did not think to have someone tell you long ago. What Amelia is experiencing—and what you will, too, in only a short time, Anne—is a normal part of growing up and becoming a woman."

Lady Juliet sat back and smiled to herself. She had told the girls much the same herself, but hearing it from the father they now adored would completely reassure them. One had to admire the deft way he handled an awkward situation. She realized that under that mocking, sophisticated front he showed the world, the duke was not only competent, he was kind.

15

The duke said no more on the subject; instead, he began to talk to Lady Juliet, and the twins were able to relax. But before many minutes had passed, he could tell from their knitted brows and unusual silence that they were deep in thought.

Then Amelia said, almost absently, "But I still don't understand. You mean that from now on until . . ." Flushing, she fell silent again.

"It doesn't seem at all fair to me! After all, boys don't . . ." Anne burst out, a mile later.

"Are you sure, Juliet?" Amelia begged as they swept through Thatcham. "Every single . . . I mean . . ."

The duke managed to ignore all these inconclusive outbursts, until Anne said in an annoyed voice, "Well, as far as I am concerned, I don't think it is a good thing to be born a female at all. Not only do we have to *marry* someone, we have to put up with . . ."

As her voice died away, the duke banged on the roof of the coach. Lady Juliet and the twins looked at him, a question in their eyes as the coachman pulled the horses to a halt.

"I am sure you will excuse me, m'ladies. It is plain to see I am *de trop,*" he said calmly as he prepared to open the door. "I will ride the groom's horse and he can join the others on the perch." There was a stunned silence, and he added, "That way, being alone, one of you might be able to finish a sentence and have some hope of a reply."

As he ducked his head to leave the coach, he caught sight of Lady Juliet's amused eyes, and he wished he might shake her. And then, as he waited for the groom to bring the horse forward, he realized that that was the last thing he wanted to do. What he wanted was to be alone with her where they might enjoy a good laugh together at this whole preposterous situation. And he wanted to thank her as well for helping him and the twins, and for being the wonderful, caring woman she was.

As the miles to Reading passed, he often stole a glance into the carriage he was riding beside. He could see the three ladies were having an intense conversation. At one point, he saw Lady Juliet lean forward and catch up both his daughters' hands where they sat across from her, to speak to them earnestly and at length. She smiled and nodded as she finished, and he saw Anne and Amelia looked a little more at ease with this awful affliction all women were condemned to suffer.

It was full dark when they reached the Reading Arms, and everyone was glad to climb down and stretch tired, cramped muscles. The duke commanded three private bedchambers, the landlord's best parlor, and an excellent dinner to be served as soon as possible, as well as food and accommodations for his servants and the horses. Then he escorted his little band up the stairs and bowed and left them alone to wash and freshen up.

When Juliet came into the private parlor some half hour later, she had an arm around each twin. They both looked more interested in the delicious aromas emanating from the sideboard than they did in making their curtsy to their father. The duke brought them sharply to order before he escorted Lady Juliet to the seat opposite his and indicated the twins were to sit on either side.

Juliet would have been content to drink her soup and relax. It had been quite a day, and now it was almost over, she was feeling weary as well as relieved. But with the inn servants in the room, conversation of necessity had to be general, and the brunt of it fell to her and the duke. As course succeeded course, she played her part, discussing plays she had seen, the current fashions, and the pleasant October weather. The duke was equally urbane, although she thought he seemed a little abstracted.

During the dessert course, he saw Anne helping herself to far too much cream for her sweet, and he would have admonished her, except the Lady Juliet was before him. He admired the one, quick glance with which she conveyed to his daughter her maladroitness, and he noticed how quickly Anne put the cream pitcher down without a word. What a domestic scene, he thought as he sipped his wine. To anyone coming into the parlor, we must appear a normal, happy family. And then an arrested look came into his eyes, and his glance went to Lady Juliet's face. Why not? he thought to himself. Why don't I marry her? She was leaning toward Amelia now, listening to some story the girl was telling her, and quite undetected, he admired her attractive, animated face, those thick lashes and hazel eyes, and the intriguing mole beside her mouth.

"Don't you think so, Father?" Amelia asked, interrupting his musings.

The duke brought himself back to the company at hand. "I beg your pardon, Amelia. I was not attending," he said, nodding to the inn servant to refill his glass. "To tell the truth, I was considering what unexpected turns fate decrees our lives should take."

Before Amelia could ask for an explanation, he changed the subject.

The twins did not linger in the parlor after dinner, for they were exhausted from the activity and emotions of the day. For a little while, they sat on either side of the fireplace, relating their adventures, but it was not long before Anne was stifling her yawns and Amelia's eyelids began to droop.

The duke rose from the table where he had chosen to

remain seated, and went to draw them both to their feet. "Go to bed, m'ladies," he said, giving them each a hug. "We have a long drive tomorrow, and there will be plenty of time to regale me with your desperate flight then."

Neither girl demurred, and they made their curtsies to Lady Juliet. "I shall come in in a little while to say good night," she told them with a smile.

The twins had almost reached the parlor door when the duke said, "Of course I hesitate to mention such a mundane subject, but I must ask you to return the money you took from my strongbox."

At that, Anne spun around, her hand going to her mouth. "I forgot all about it!" she cried. "I'll get it at once, sir."

The duke waved a dismissing hand. "I do not need it until tomorrow," he told them. The twins waited, looking puzzled. "You see, without that money, my dears, we have no way to pay our shot here. When you took it, you effectively impoverished me. And I do not think we would care to work out the bill, I as an ostler, perhaps the Lady Juliet serving lager and ale in the taproom, and you two laboring as the scullery maids you once thought it preferable to be."

Juliet was still smiling as the echo of the girls' laughter faded away down the passageway, and then she came and took her seat again, wishing she might have excused herself as well. She stole a glance at the duke, to find him staring into the fire, his chin propped up on one long, elegant hand. A little smile played around the corners of his mouth, and she wondered if he had read her mind and knew she was dreading being alone with him.

After a moment's silence, he stood up and went to the decanter on the sideboard. "Let me pour you a glass of wine, Lady Juliet," he said, his voice courteous. Juliet would have denied him, but he went on smoothly,

"There is no way I—indeed, all the Fairhavens—can thank you for what you did today. And I am reminded that this is not the first time that you have come to the aid of my tiresome brats. You are too good!"

He came and handed her the glass, and she made herself smile slightly, willing him to move away again. "There is no need for your gratitude, sir. The girls are my dear friends, and I have always found them delightful."

The duke shook his head a little as he sat down across from her and leaned back at his ease. "You can still say that after today, and all the other contretemps they have managed to embroil you in?" he asked, his drawl incredulous.

Juliet sipped her wine. "But of course. These things are merely the mishaps all youth is prone to; they will outgrow such starts before long." She stopped, and then she looked into the fire as she said, "And you yourself do not really consider them 'tiresome brats.' In fact, I know you have a great deal of affection for them now, do you not? One might almost say, a deep love. Why else would you be so concerned for them and their well-being?"

The duke smiled, admiring her profile, and the way the firelight lit the blond threads in her hair and turned them to pure gold. "I beg you to keep that secret, m'lady," he drawled. "How dreadful if the Dreadful Duke should earn a reputation as an easily gulled dupe. I should never live it down."

Juliet laughed at his shocked tone and turned to look at him, her smile lighting her expressive eyes. "You have not been the Dreadful Duke for some time, sir. And it would take a colder man than you are not to love the twins. They have such charm and warmth. But although it makes me a traitor to my sex, I should point out to you that you are in serious danger of being wrapped around two identical adolescent fingers. 'Ware entrapment, sir! You have been warned."

William Fairhaven chuckled. "I know. I did not realize the extend of my bewitchment until I learned that they had run away to save me from the Black Plague." Suddenly he gave a shout of laughter. "The Black Plague! And then riding to Bath to drink the waters! Wherever did they think they would stay, two young girls alone?"

Juliet joined his laughter, but it died in her throat as he added in a different, more serious tone, "Strange, is it not? I find myself bewitched by so many ladies of late. Do you think perhaps my carefully preserved indifference is failing me?"

At that, Juliet rose and smoothed her skirts. "You must excuse me, your Grace," she said, looking straight into his gleaming dark eyes. The duke rose as well, and she hurried on, "I promised to look in on the girls before they went to sleep. And then I think I shall retire as well. It has been a long day."

The duke came toward her, shaking his head. "Retire at nine o'clock?" he asked, his voice mocking. "Surely you would not condemn me to such a long, solitary evening, m'lady. No, no, I must insist that you return."

He took up her hand to hold it in both of his, his clasp warm as he added, "There is something I want to discuss with you, Lady Juliet, and I can assure you it is important. Pray humor me in this instance."

His intent eyes held hers, and at last, in desperation to get away from his disturbing nearness, she nodded. "Of course, your Grace. I shall be with you presently."

The duke released her hand and she went to the door, trying not to hurry her steps.

She found the twins fast asleep in the big four-poster in the room, looking as innocent as two babies in the soft glow of the firelight. Juliet adjusted their covers and dropped a light kiss on each brow before she turned away to go and stand before the hearth.

She knew she must go back to the duke; she could not escape him. She told herself she must be cool, casual, and very, very proper. He would follow her lead; he was a gentleman, after all. And then she laughed at herself. A gentleman? Oh, yes, and she knew all about them, did she not? The Duke of Severn was no better, and no worse, than any other man, but because she realized this, she would be on her guard. Besides, he could hardly force any lovemaking on her, here in a crowded inn with his daughters sleeping right next door. She was fearing a danger that did not exist, behaving like a silly, stupid girl.

Tilting her chin, she picked up her skirt and went out the door, closing it softly behind her. Even so, with all her resolution, she could not help looking back at her own bedroom door with longing. There was sanctuary; ahead, as she was all too well aware, lay danger.

As she entered the private parlor again, the duke came to lead her back to her seat by the fire, asking after the twins as he did so. Juliet was glad when he returned to his own place across from her, and she drew a deep breath.

"You said there was something you wanted to speak to me about, your Grace?" she asked, her voice cool.

"There is indeed, my dear," William Fairhaven told her. "I want to ask you to do me the honor of marrying me."

Juliet could not stifle a gasp of astonishment. "Marrying you?" she whispered, one hand going to her throat. The duke admired her wide, startled eyes and that half-open mouth that was trembling with shock, his glance almost proprietary.

He nodded. "Marrying me. I would, of course, prefer to take you in my arms so I might show you my eagerness for such a union, but from past experience I know that would not be acceptable to you. And so I am forced to tell you how much I revere you, verbally. I pray my powers of persuasion do not forsake me."

Juliet continued to stare at him. She could not read any sarcasm either in his voice or on his face; indeed, both were carefully expressionless. She wondered at it, thinking frantically. "Why?" she blurted out, and then inwardly cursed herself for her gaucheness.

"Why does any man want to marry a woman, ma'am?" he countered, as if pondering a serious question. His dark eyes seemed to grow keener as he leaned forward and added softly, "I find I began by admiring you and all your qualities, but now I want to spend the rest of my life with you. I do not know if that is love, I only know I must have you beside me for my future happiness and peace of mind."

"Are you sure you are not asking me just to gain a mother for the twins, sir?" Juliet asked when she could speak over the rapid pulse that was beating in her throat.

The duke stiffened and his expression grew haughty. "Are you determined to insult not only me, but yourself as well, madam?" he asked. "I have been a widower for thirteen years. If I felt the twins needed a mother so badly, surely I would have married long before now." He shook his head. "No, I find I want you for myself, and I want you as soon as the matter can be arranged."

Juliet hoped he did not see the shiver she felt run through her body. He did not say another word, but he never took those dark, compelling eyes from hers. Mesmerized, she stared back, and then, as the silence between them lengthened, she said in a voice that was little more than a croak, "No."

One slashing brow rose abruptly, and she was recalled to her manners. "I must beg your pardon, your Grace. Of course I am greatly conscious of the honor you do me, but I cannot accept your proposal."

"Why not?" the duke asked, swinging one booted foot gently. His voice was quiet and controlled, and she could read no disappointment in it.

"Because, as I have told you before, I have no desire to marry, ever. Not—not anyone."

"But I am not just *anyone,* my dear Juliet. I am Severn," he reminded her, his voice arrogant now. Then he added, "Ah, yes, your so-called antipathy for men. But don't you think that in time you might conquer that dislike, my dear? You would only have to love *one* of the species, for I should be delighted if you continued to hold the rest of my sex in aversion."

A little devilish light of amusement shone in his eyes, and she swallowed hard. "No," she said again, more firmly now. "Not now, and not ever."

It seemed an age that they remained silent, their eyes locked, and then the duke said softly, "You do see that you must tell me why you have this hatred for men and why you feel you can never marry me. I think you owe me that much, ma'am, and it is the only way you can convince me."

Juliet rose in some agitation when she saw the challenge in his eyes. She took a deep breath and then she said, "Very well. You have badgered and bothered me almost the entire time I have known you. I never meant to tell another living soul, but I will tell you, your Grace, if only to show you most clearly why any alliance with your sex will always be repugnant to me. Indeed, after you hear me out, you will be glad I refused you."

She paused for a moment and then she said, "It is a long story, and not a pleasant one, I fear."

The duke watched her as she paced the room, a frown on her face, as if she were gathering her thoughts, and he said, "I should be honored to hear your story, Juliet, and you may be sure I shall keep whatever you tell me in confidence."

As if his voice broke some spell, she turned and gave a bitter laugh. "Oh, I do pray you will do that, sir! I should hardly care to have it bruited about after all this time. Why, no one in England knows, and if they should learn it, I would be ruined indeed."

She clasped her hands before her, and keeping her eyes on his, she began, "My mother and I sailed for America in the spring of 1804. Our journey was uneventful, and by autumn we were living at Belle-manoir, my aunt and uncle's estate. They called themselves Mr. and Mrs. LaFontaine then. Their plantation was located some twenty miles northeast of New Orleans, on Lake Pontchartrain. It was a beautiful spot, and my mother soon ceased to mourn my father when she was swept up into the society of the day and the luxuries my uncle's wealth could provide. But even then, long before the war, there were those Americans who hated the British. Many of them had grown up during the earlier revolution and had lost an older brother or a father to British guns."

She stopped and waved an impatient hand. "Forgive me. I am sure you do not need the history lesson, your Grace."

The duke would have spoken, but she hurried on, "In spite of all those who considered us their enemies, many still were kind to us, for my uncle's sake. He had renounced his allegiance to France to become an American, you see.

"But the hatred, although hidden away, was always there, as I was to discover. After a few years, I—I fell in love with the son of a neighboring plantation owner. We had not met before because he was the captain of a vessel that traded between Europe and the new southern states."

Here Juliet paused. The duke watched her pale face, and the way she swallowed, but he did not interrupt. So far, it seemed a fairly ordinary little tale; he could write the ending to it even now, and he wondered why it had overset her so much.

"He loved me too, at least he said he did," she added with a little grimace. "He spoke to my mother and gained her permission easily, but my uncle would not consent to our marriage until his friend and neighbor, the captain's father, also agreed."

The duke saw the way Juliet's hazel eyes darkened with pain.

"It was then that I discovered how deep the roots of hatred could go. His father, who had always been pleasant to me, not only forbade our marriage, he threatened to disinherit his son if he persisted in it. He told him that any alliance with an Englishwoman would ruin his life and place him under the same stigma with which I was regarded. And then he told him how the captain's own uncle had been tortured by the Indians during the Revolution, and how his grave had been desecrated by British dragoons. You must understand, your Grace, I learned all this when my fiancé came to explain to me why our marriage was not possible."

She stopped for a moment to recover her composure, and the duke asked, "How old was this captain of your, Juliet?"

"He was twenty-nine," she said, sounding surprised at the question.

"One would think that was old enough to know his own mind and damn the consequences, if he could win *you,*" the duke drawled. "But do go on."

Juliet shrugged. "Perhaps he was weak. Yes, I see now he must have been. Or perhaps the undying love he claimed to have for me was not quite as compelling as he thought." She shrugged. "Suffice to say, he married shortly thereafter, a lovely young lady of American parentage, who had the added advantage of being the only child of an extremely well-to-do shipowner."

The duke rose and poured her a glass of wine, and as he handed it to her, he said, "Drink this, my dear. All this must have been very distressing for you, but I hardly think it cause to hate all men forevermore. Your captain was only one, and a very weak reed at that. All men are not like him. Perhaps you came to that conclusion too quickly?"

Juliet's smile was ironic. "My story is not told, your Grace. Pray wait until you hear the end before you decide I was unfair."

The duke nodded as he took his seat again, and waited for her to continue.

"My mother took the captain's jilting very badly. She said she had been humiliated beyond belief, and after a while, she would not even appear in public again. Without her parties and calls and teas, she had little with which to occupy herself, and so she began to imagine she was ill. She had spells of hysteria, and she never stopped reminding me that her exile from all the pleasant pastimes she had formerly enjoyed was all my fault."

The duke shook his head, his expression bleak as he contemplated the shallow woman Juliet's mother had been. Had she ever even considered how much more painful this must have been to a young woman in love?

"And then," Juliet went on, breaking into his thoughts, "late one afternoon when I was returning home from a solitary ride, I was waylaid by a masked man."

"A highwayman?" the duke asked, his voice disbelieving.

Juliet shook her head, and the duke saw that the hands she had clasped in her lap were white with tension.

"The highwayman was none other than my gallant captain," she said, her voice colorless. "He had been drinking, and he had convinced himself that I was

199

indeed his enemy. I learned later that two of his father-in-law's ships had been captured by the British in the Caribbean, not that that excuses what he did."

She raised her chin and looked straight into his eyes as she said clearly, "You see, he raped me."

William Fairhaven sat frozen as her hands came up to knead her temples and her hazel eyes grew distant with memory. "I shall never forget that afternoon as long as I live," she said softly. "He stopped me in a lonely part of the estate. There was no sense in calling for help, although I did. But he just pulled me from my horse and carried me into the woods. I can still hear him laughing at my attempts to fight him off, and the curses and obscenities he yelled as he pushed me to the ground and tore at my clothes. Sometimes I can still feel that hard ground bruising my skin and smell the heavy scent of the grass and the wild flowers that were crushed beneath me. I shall never forget it, never!"

She shuddered, and then she made a conscious effort to regain her composure. The duke had risen and was coming toward her, but she warded him off with her hands. "Do not touch me," she said quickly, loathing in every syllable. "No man touches me anymore!"

The duke stopped, horror and distaste written plain on his stern face. Juliet nodded a little, as if she had been expecting just such a reaction, but when he would have spoken, she held up a deterring hand before she lowered her eyes to her lap.

"Please let me finish, your Grace, lest I never do so at all." She took a deep breath and then she continued, "That experience was terrible beyond imagining, but because of it there was worse to come. My mother, on learning of the rape, went completely out of her mind. She pretended I was invisible, almost as if she had never had a daughter at all. And yet I was the one who had to care for her in her madness. My aunt refused to have anything more to do with her, claiming her own nerves would not stand the strain."

"My dear Juliet," the duke began, as if he could remain silent no longer, but when she raised her eyes to his face and he saw the naked pain in them, he fell silent.

"My attacker was never punished, of course. I told my uncle who he was, but he refused to accuse him and bring him to justice. It would have made his life there impossible, and we both knew it. Besides, Bellemanoir was far more important to him than any niece by marriage." Juliet stopped and raised her handkerchief to her lips.

After a moment, she went on, her voice quieter now, "Somehow people found out about the rape. I suspect the captain could not resist bragging about how he had punished and humiliated a British subject. My aunt was horrified, and she insisted that my mother and I remove from the mansion. From that time on, we lived alone in a small cottage out of sight and hearing of the main house. My uncle gave me two strong slaves to help me. You see, my mother had to be restrained lest she do herself or someone else an injury in her madness."

The duke saw how she was twisting her handkerchief in her hands, and then she sighed and said, "My story is almost told, your Grace. Two years ago, my mother died of typhoid, and I was free at last to return to England. Since we were at war with the United States then, I had to leave the country any way I could. My uncle was instrumental in my success. And on my long, roundabout voyage home, I came to understand and accept the only life that was left to me. I was the Lady Juliet Manchester still, and that was all I ever could be, or wanted to be. I would tell no one of my ordeal and my shame, and I would never, ever, let a man into my life again."

She sighed, and she unclasped her hands and rubbed them as if to bring the blood back in circulation, and then, lifting her head proudly, she said, "And now you have finally uncovered my sordid little past, your Grace. Knowing what you do now, I am sure you can see why any liaison between us is not possible."

"You said earlier that no one in England knows," the duke remarked, his voice matter-of-fact. "Do you mean you have not told the Reverend Manchester?"

Juliet shook her head. "No, I could not tell even him."

"But he is a parson and your brother," the duke said. "Surely he would have understood, helped to comfort you—"

"No!" Juliet cried. "I could not bear for him to know! It was such a relief when I returned here to anonymity after being treated like a pariah, a whore." She stopped, her voice little more than a choked, anguished whisper now.

The duke rose quickly, and before she knew it, he was beside her, his hands pulling her into his arms with one, fluid motion. Juliet raised her own hands and began to push him away, a sob coming to her throat at her helplessness. She realized he was too strong for her to repulse, even as she wondered why he had taken her in his arms at all. Dear God, hadn't he heard her? Then she was surprised when his hands released their pressure a little, and she was quick to try to draw away again.

"Do not fight me, Juliet," Willliam Fairhaven said, bending down to whisper in her ear. She thought his voice sounded strained and ragged as he continued. "You have had a terrible time and you have been through so much alone. I find it hard to understand how you ever survived, never mind remained the lovely woman that you are. Let me hold you close and comfort you, as I might hold the twins when they are hurt."

For a moment, Juliet remained stiff with tension, and

then she put her head on his chest and sighed. She closed her eyes, grateful for his warm, consoling arms, the first she had known since that awful afternoon.

His hands were gentle on her back, and one came up to cradle her head, his fingers pushing her hair aside so he might stroke the back of her neck. Her own hands rested on his broad chest, and she could feel the steady thudding of his heart as it beat strongly next to her ear. He did not speak, and she was grateful.

She realized she was drawing more comfort from his warm strength than she would have from a thousand reassuring words. She felt herself relaxing, becoming limp and weak. As she sagged in his arms, they tightened to keep her safe. And then, all at once, she felt tears clogging her throat and stinging her eyelids, those tears she had promised herself she would never shed again.

The duke felt her stir a little, but when he would have drawn back to look down into her eyes, her hands moved to grasp his lapels so she might hide her face. "Please do not say anything now, your Grace," she begged in a broken voice. "Let me go . . . don't look at me!"

"My dear Juliet, it is not the insurmountable disaster that you think," he began, but he could feel her twist her head in negation.

Then she said passionately, "No, no more! I cannot bear it!"

He let her go then, for he had heard how close she was to hysteria. Without meeting his eyes or saying another word, she ran from the room.

16

For several minutes, William Fairhaven remained standing where Juliet had left him. He was not only stunned but shaken by what she had told him. Indeed, if it had been anyone but the Lady Juliet Manchester, he would not have believed such a magnitude of disasters. But she had spoken so matter-of-factly, it was apparent that all the horrible, humiliating episodes that she had related were true. No wonder she hated men!

At last he ran a hand over his dark hair and went to sit by the fire again. He knew there was no sense in going to bed, for he would not be able to sleep. Instead, he let his mind range back over her story. Even as starkly as she had told it, he could see in vivid detail the scenes she had painted, and experience the emotions she had felt. First, the weak, shallow man who had given her up without even a struggle, and who had married wealth and an assured future only a short time later. This was not surprising; the duke knew how many selfish people there were in the world. That Juliet had thought she loved him mattered little. She had been young then and no doubt overwhelmed by her first feelings of passion. And of course the captain must have been handsome and charming, with the added attraction of an exotic career. The duke was aware how often young women were swayed by a uniform and drawn to men who lived in danger.

He tried very hard not to dwell on the subsequent rape. Juliet had not described it in any detail, but his imagination told him only too clearly what it must have been like. How terrible it must have been to be attacked by a man she had once loved! Now he knew why she had been so distraught when he had asked her to speak to the twins about rapists. If only he had known!

William Fairhaven grimaced, his face taut with agony. He could easily picture that weak man who had drunk enough to convince himself that Juliet was his enemy and, as such, must be punished in the most humiliating way a man could punish a woman. Or perhaps he had still been attracted to her physically, in spite of his marriage to the American heiress, and calling her his enemy had been only an excuse to enjoy what he had been forced to give up. But no, he told himself, he must not dwell on that possibility, for that way lay madness. But that a drunken animal had hurt and disgraced someone as fine as Juliet made him want to put his head back and howl with rage. He rose to pace the room for a moment, his black brows forming a ferocious bar across his forehead, and his mouth set like stone. He was helpless. He could not even punish the man as he deserved, not now. It had happened years ago, and all he could do now was curse him, damning him to eternal hellfire.

To calm himself, he tried to recall what he knew of Louisiana. He had stayed there for a few weeks several years ago, and he was familiar with the type of people she had described, their vast plantations and pretentious mansions. He cast his mind back over the slow-moving circle of endless parties and picnics and balls, the little group of well-to-do landowners and their families who considered themselves the elite and who watched one another so carefully. It was often so in insular places. What had happened to Juliet, and her mother's retreat into madness, would never be forgotten, no matter that she herself was blameless. They were at heart a narrow, puritanical people, jealous of their importance and status. That Juliet had been English only made it easier for them to despise her.

He sighed. There was nothing he could do to erase what had happened to her abroad, but he promised himself he would make it up to her if it took the rest of his life to do so. It was strange. He had not felt anything but pity for her as she told the story, nor did he as he recalled it now. He had meant it when he had said he did not know how she had remained the wonderful woman she was, in the face of such adversity. Why, she had accepted her uncle's unwillingness to bring her attacker to justice, her aunt's abandonment, and the years she had spent caring for a madwoman without becoming bitter. By living through all that hellish time and maintaining her own standards and decency while doing so, she became even finer in his eyes, and infinitely more dear.

He was glad he had proposed so precipitously, for in doing so he had forced her to a confession at last, and he was proud that he was the one person in England she had told. She would not have done so if she had not felt he could be trusted with her secret.

But then he remembered that he had asked her to marry him mainly to gain a mother for his twins, or so he had thought. He had liked and admired her, for she was agreeable and lovely, and he had been sure they would deal very well together. Now he knew it was more than that, much more indeed. It had to be, for that William Fairhaven, the proud and arrogant Duke of Severn, to still want a woman who had suffered what Juliet had, made it only too clear how much he cared for her. Not as a mother for his twins or a conformable wife, as gracious and pleasant as Anne had been, but as his own dearest Juliet. It was as if her confession had swept aside a dense veil, showing him the depths of his love for her at last.

He told himself he must make sure she knew how strong his love was, in spite of her past. She had run away before he could reassure her, and he had not attempted to delay her, for he sensed how much she needed to be alone then, but he took it as a very good sign that she had let him hold her at the end. His face brightened for the first time in an hour. How wonderful she had felt in his arms. And he knew she was not a cold woman, no matter what she claimed. Her revulsion for the male sex was only the result of the pain one man had brought her. He had felt her trembling, not only tonight but on other occasions, and he sensed it was not only from fear, but from desire as well. When they were married, he would show her how wonderful the act of love could be with all the gentle, patient persuasion he could bring to bear, and he would not hurry her, no matter how long it took. Juliet's happiness was worth any effort of his, for he knew now he could never be content if she were not.

He rose then and stretched. It was very late; the inn had been quiet for a long time. He would go to bed, and tomorrow he would begin his courtship in earnest. And then he warned himself that it might be better to allow her a little time to recover her poise. She was sure to be embarrassed at first meeting, and he did not want to upset her, especially in front of the twins. As he made his way to his room, he told himself he must return to his former manner until he had restored Juliet to her aunt's house in London. But then he would act quickly and with resolve. He paused at her door, one hand going involuntarily to the door knob, and he smiled. How he wished he was twenty—and Juliet eighteen! If that had been the case, he would have gone to her now, full of impatient ardor, to kiss and caress her until she was forced to admit her love for him as well. Unfortunately, he was not twenty, and he had learned prudence. He would wait—but only for her sake.

Juliet was surprised to find she slept very well that night. When she had first reached her room, she had thrown herself down on the bed and wept as she had not wept in years. It was as if the tears washed away a hitherto impregnable high wall, leaving her soft and open and defenseless. When she sat up and wiped her eyes at last, she experienced a calm she had never known as well. She undressed quickly and was soon snuggling under the warm quilts, her eyes heavy with weariness and her soul at peace. It seemed that telling the duke the story she had kept locked away in the dark recesses of her mind for such a long time had released her from its power to hurt her anymore.

In the morning, she was not so sanguine. She lingered in her room as long as she dared, for she was reluctant to face him and see how he would react to her presence. She was sure that the story she had told him would cause him to treat her with barely concealed revulsion, and that once he had returned her to London, he would be quick to cut the connection. She would not be at all surprised if he never permitted her to see the twins again. She put up her chin, but she was careful not to look into her own eyes as she peered into the dim mirror to do up her hair.

The twins knocked soon afterward, demanding to know what was taking her so long, and their chatter as they led her to the private parlor for breakfast enabled her to present a calm front she was far from feeling. The duke rose as she entered, his dark eyes searching her face.

"Good morning, Lady Juliet," he said formally, coming to hold her chair. "I hope you slept well?"

Juliet stole a glance at his face. William Fairhaven did not look as if he himself had slept very well. There were deep-etched lines on his face, and his eyes held a little frown. She felt despair wash over her, even as she told herself it was just what she had expected.

"Very well, thank you, your Grace," she made herself say. Fortunately, Anne interrupted this stilted conversation by asking if she cared for eggs or for fish.

"And there some delicious muffins, too," Anne assured her.

Juliet allowed the girl to serve her, although she felt she could hardly swallow a mouthful, even after the duke excused himself almost immediately, saying he must make sure the carriage was ready.

As he went out, Amelia scowled down at her plate and Juliet had to ask her what the matter was.

"Father seems so stern, so distant," the girl complained. "It must be because we ran away, but I do not understand it. He was kind to us yesterday."

"Perhaps his bed was lumpy," Anne remarked, chasing the last little bit of egg around her plate with her fork.

Juliet thought to ask Amelia how she was feeling then, and the dangerous subject that was the Duke of Severn was forgotten.

When the three came down to the carriage, the girls were disappointed to learn that their father was going to ride the mare to London.

"But we won't say a word about—about *that,* Father," Anne promised him.

"Not a single word!" Amelia added.

The duke smiled at them. "I am sure you will not, but I have a fancy to ride. It is a lovely day, perhaps one of the last good days we shall have before the winter storms begin. The Little Season is almost over."

He came to help Juliet to her seat in the carriage, and she forced herself to keep her face expressionless as she felt his steadying hand under her arm. She nodded to thank him, for she did not feel she could speak, but she did not look at him. That was unfortunate, for the duke was gazing at her with all the love he felt for her shining in his eyes.

Juliet was abstracted on the return journey, and Anne and Amelia exchanged glances and unspoken comments. They tried to question her, but when Lady Juliet was set down in Chesterfield Street early that afternoon, they were no wiser than before.

As the carriage continued on to Berkeley Square, Anne said, "I wonder what has happened to Juliet? She was so pale and stiff. Why, she almost looked just like Father does today!"

Amelia nodded. "It does not seem as if things are going very well between them, does it? Maybe they had an argument after we went to bed last night."

"It is too bad," Anne complained. "And just when we thought it was only the matter of a short time before they would be married, too."

Her twin nodded, and then she said, "I never realized it took so long, this marrying business. I mean, once you know you like someone, what can possibly delay things?"

"I wish we could ask Father why he doesn't propose," Anne said, and then she began to laugh. Amelia was quick to join her, for she could picture, as well as her twin could, the impossibility of them ever approaching that proud, formal gentleman to inquire about his love life.

The duke was glad to see them in such good spirits, for they were still giggling as they tumbled out of the carriage at journey's end. Then he excused himself without entering the house, saying he had an errand to do. The twins looked at him, stunned. Go out without bathing and changing? It was most unlike the fastidious Duke of Severn.

William Fairhaven returned to Berkeley Square a short time later, but by that time the girls were in the schoolroom, regaling their governess with their adventures. He had only gone as far as the nearest florist to make arrangements for a large bouquet to be delivered to Lady Juliet as soon as possible. Now, he shut himself up in the library to compose a letter to her, the most important letter he had never penned in his life. He found it more than just difficult; he found it impossible. He did not want to tell her the things in his heart on paper; he wanted to hold her close and whisper them in her ear. And so page after page of elegant crested paper found itself flung into the fire, and it was over an hour later before the duke came back to the hall and handed his butler a short note to be delivered to the lady at once.

Juliet had opened the card that accompanied her flowers with nerveless fingers. She was disappointed to discover there was no personal message on the duke's calling card, and then she took herself to task for being so foolish as to expect one. It was obvious that the bouquet was only a polite acknowledgment of her help, a courtesy that someone as polished as the duke would scorn to forget, no matter what his feelings for the recipient might be.

Lady Elizabeth, seated across from her, watched her niece with shrewd eyes, but she was quick to bend her head over her tambour frame when Juliet raised her head. The older lady had had the tale of the twins' latest misadventure, and although she had exclaimed and laughed until the tears ran down her cheeks, she had not missed the little hesitation before Juliet spoke of the duke, nor the way her face had paled when she mentioned his name. Lady Elizabeth made some plans of her own, then.

When the duke's note was delivered some time later, Lady Elizabeth had left the drawing room, and so she did not know how Juliet reacted to this latest communication. She might not have been surprised if she could have seen how eagerly Juliet read it, not once but several times, but she would have been amazed at the way her niece rose so quickly to go and fling it into the fire, her head held high and her lips compressed.

211

The duke, unwilling to make love to her on paper, had written only to ask for an interview in the morning. The note was formal and terse, without so much as a hint of the lover. He had even signed it with his full title, and as Juliet climbed the stairs, she told herself it could just as well have been written to his vintner or his tailor.

It was just what she had anticipated. No doubt he felt he had to call in order to thank her in person, and perhaps he even felt bound as a gentleman to repeat his proposal. Well, it was unfortunate he had to spend another worrisome night, but by tomorrow he could be calm. Her second refusal would most certainly release him from the obligation. How relieved he would be! She had no interest in her toilette that evening, and she was glad that for once she and her aunt were dining at home alone.

When the duke arrived the next morning, he was surprised to find not Juliet waiting for him, but the Lady Elizabeth Pettibone instead. He checked at the door of the drawing room for a moment as the butler announced him, and then he came forward to bow and take the lady's hand up to kiss.

"Not whom you expected to see, I daresay, Severn," Lady Elizabeth told him in her positive way, looking with a jaundiced eye at his tall, well-built figure in its charcoal-gray coat from Weston, clinging pearl-gray breeches, and pristine white linen. "I want a few words with you, my good man."

"But I shall be delighted, as always, to exchange as many words as you like, ma'am. I am at your service," the duke said smoothly. Lady Elizabeth sniffed and waved him to a seat.

"What happened to Juliet on your rescue mission?" his hostess began, as always getting right to the heart of the matter.

"Happened?" the duke asked, one black brow quirked in inquiry. "Why do you think something happened?" His voice was bland and his face carefully cool and contained.

Lady Elizabeth wished she might shake him. "I am not blind, nor simple," she told him tartly. "Juliet came back here with a lost, hurt look in her eyes. And although I made no demur at the time—indeed, it was not in my power to do so, for although I am her aunt, I have no control over her actions, not at her age—I find it very singular that she went haring off with you, unchaperoned and carrying an overnight bag. I would be well within my rights as an older member of the family if I insisted you marry her, sir! In fact, now that I think it over, I *do* insist. The Manchesters are of the nobility; Juliet's reputation is not to be sullied even by someone as exalted as the Duke of Severn. You will do your duty and offer the gel marriage—and at once!"

Her voice was militant and her gray eyes snapped as she settled back to await his reaction to this ultimatum.

"Your concern for the lady is quite unnecessary, ma'am," the duke told her, amusement filling his dark eyes and a smile curling his mouth. Lady Elizabeth thought him much too nonchalant for the seriousness of the situation, but his next words banished all thoughts of telling him so from her mind.

"I have already asked the Lady Juliet to marry me. Not because I had to, mind you, but because I wanted to," the duke told her. Lady Elizabeth's mouth fell open in surprise.

"So far she had denied me," he went on, "but I hope to change her mind in a very short time."

Lady Elizabeth had to laugh. His voice had been so urbane, so assured and positive, she knew he could not envision being refused. And, she had to admit, it would be a very strange sort of female who could say no to the tall, handsome, magnetic person who was the Duke of Severn.

She rose and shook out her skirts, and the duke rose

as well. "Then there is nothing further to discuss. I shall send her to you at once, and may I be the first to wish you happy, even though I am slightly premature, William?" she asked.

She barely waited for the duke's bow before she hurried from the room, a beaming smile on her face.

When Juliet came in, she found the duke standing before the fireplace. His dark eyes studied her face as she came toward him. He did not think she looked well, for above her elegant green morning gown with its gay knots of ribbons, her face was pale and set. She wore her hair pulled back in a severe chignon, and he could tell from the tilt of her head and the careful, controlled look in her eyes that she had herself well in hand.

"*My* lady," he said, coming to take her hand.

Juliet curtsied, lowering her eyes for a moment at the distinction those two separate words conferred. She told herself she must take care not to show any reaction to them, but when she raised her eyes to his again, she could not restrain a tiny gasp. He was smiling down at her so tenderly, and with such warmth.

"I trust you have recovered from the trauma of our journey, ma'am?" the duke asked, still holding her hand in his.

Juliet pulled it away and went to sit on the stiffest chair in the room. The duke took the one across from her after moving it forward until their knees were almost touching.

"Thank you, your Grace," she made herself say. "I am quite recovered."

"Please call me William, my dear," he told her. "After all, I *have* proposed to you, so this formality you practice is a little excessive."

"But I denied you, sir," Juliet began.

The duke held up his hand. "Then you must know I shall continue to ask for your hand until you grow so tired of refusing that you will marry me simply in order to change the subject," he told her, amusement brimming in his eyes.

Juliet stiffened. She could feel her heart begin to pound and her hands grow damp as she studied his face. Although she looked closely, she could not see the slightest reluctance, nor the tiniest hint of revulsion. He was a consummate actor indeed, for there was nothing written there but a fervent desire for their marriage.

"You will grow weary of asking, long before I change my mind, your Grace," she said through stiff lips. "Indeed, it is very good of you to continue to behave as if our marriage is your fondest wish, but you see, I do not believe you."

She rose then and walked away from him, her head bowed. Then she turned and said, "You are the Duke of Severn. I know how proud you are of your name, your heritage. That is how it should be. It would be a travesty of everything you believe in and hold dear for you to marry such a woman as I have become. If you do wed again, it should be to someone who is your equal—a pure, refined lady with impeccable bloodlines who is untouched by even a breath of scandal."

"I married someone like that years ago when I was very young. As young as you were when you fell in love with the dastardly captain," the duke told her as he came toward her. Juliet thought his voice had hardened a bit, and she wondered at it. "Our marriage, although it produced five children, was never more than just a pleasant arrangement to give Severn an heir. It was comfortable, not engrossing, friendly rather than passionate. That is not how I want you, my dear. And since I married once to fulfill society's expectations, might I not do so now to please myself?"

Juliet began to feel beleaguered, and she lashed out at him. "Is this some kind of jest with you?" she asked, her voice unsteady. "Do you have some sort of sick

215

fascination for the defiled? After what happened to me, how can you want me?''

The duke interrupted her, his voice cold. "No, Juliet, my proposal is no jest, and because of my love for you, I shall forgive your insult that I, Severn, am preoccupied with the perverse. How dare you even imply such a thing?''

His voice was harsh now and his eyes blazed, and Juliet could not help shivering a little. Then, more softly, he said, "You must believe that I want you because I love you, more than I ever expected to love anyone. You see, before I met you, I was incapable of that emotion. I shall always be grateful to you for showing me what love really is.''

Juliet backed away. It was dangerous being so close to him. "I will not marry you," she said, shaking her head. The duke came after her, and when she read the determination in his eyes, she added quickly, "Leaving my circumstances aside, you deserve someone better than a cold, fearful woman who shudders at any man's touch. I have seen the women you admire, and I—I can never be like them.''

Now his Grace was shaking his head. He was close to her again, and with a brocade sofa at her back, she could retreat no farther. He did not touch her as he bent down from his great height and said softly, "You are not cold, my dear, not at all. You are only afraid, as who would not be after enduring what you have gone through? And although it pains me to have to remind you once again, I am not just 'any man.' ''

He looked haughty for only a moment, and then he whispered, "I will show you the kind of woman you are, as loving and warm as you were always meant to be. And soon you will come to know the kind of man I can be.''

He reached out then and put his arms around her to draw her close. Juliet did not seem to be able to take her eyes from his. As before, she did not feel threatened by his touch, not even when his hands began to caress her. Giving up the struggle to bring him to his senses, she put her head on his chest and sighed. For a long moment they stood there quietly together, and then he said, his voice uneven with emotion, "My dearest Juliet, know that I love you with my entire heart, and say you will try to love me a little in return. I only ask to care for you, protect you, honor and adore you."

He moved a little then, to tilt her chin with one hand and look down into her hazel eyes which were fringed with those thick lashes tipped with gold. When he saw the doubt and fear in them, he tried to show her, by his own expression, the truth of his words. And then, very slowly, he bent his head and kissed her. It was not a passionate kiss, but rather the same kind he might have given the twins, gentle and warm and reassuring. Juliet closed her eyes and tried to will herself to remain untouched by it.

At last he raised his head and murmured, "Darling, forget what happened to you in America. It was all so long ago, in the dim and dusty past. We have a future to consider."

She opened her eyes to stare at him, and he added, "If I can forget it, why can't you?"

She caught her breath. The yearning to believe him was so strong, it was like an undertow sweeping her out to sea, and there was nothing she could do to resist it, no matter how she tried.

His hands tightened at her waist as his dark eyes searched her face. And then, as if they moved of their own volition, her arms crept up around his neck. At once, his expression brightened, and those chiseled lips that looked so stern, yet felt so warm and alive, smiled.

Juliet closed her eyes again as his mouth possessed hers for a second time. He was so gentle, so undemanding, that quite without meaning to she pressed closer to him, her hands burying themselves in his thick, dark hair.

And then the duke kissed her as he had been longing to do.

To her surprise, Juliet did not stiffen with fear. It seemed so right, so inevitable. It was almost as if she had been born only for this one perfect moment. Almost as if everything she had had to endure before had been only an unhappy prelude that she had to live through until he found her at last. By the time their lips parted, Juliet knew how much she cared for him, and he for her, and her whole being seemed to be crying out in both triumph and surrender.

The knock on the drawing-room door was a most unwelcome intrusion. Juliet drew back to smooth her gown and her hair. The duke searched her face, as if he were afraid he might find some lingering reluctance there, and when she saw his fear, Juliet gave him a tremulous smile.

"The Ladies Anne and Amelia Fairhaven, m'lady," Lady Elizabeth's butler announced, interrupting their idyll.

The twins came in, but they stopped abruptly just inside the door to stare at their father and their best friend.

"Sir! We didn't know you were here," Anne said, her voice almost accusatory.

William Fairhaven's bow was ironic. "You must forgive me, m'lady. I did not realize you required the schedule of my day's activities," he said.

Anne tilted her head. He did not sound angry, only as sarcastic as he always did, but sometimes it was hard to tell.

"Perhaps we should come back another time," Lady Amelia said, watching Juliet's face. "We would not want to interrupt anything portenous."

"Portentous," both Juliet and the duke said togther, and then they smiled at each other.

Anne squeezed her twin's hand and they ran down the drawing room to where Juliet and their father were standing close together, looking at each other as if they could not bear to stop.

"Is it true?" Anne asked eagerly. "Are you going to marry Juliet, Father?"

"Are you going to marry Father, Juliet?" Amelia asked at the same instant.

"It certainly took you enough time," Anne pointed out.

William Fairhaven tore his eyes from Juliet's lovely face. "I am, she is, and the amount of time it took is none of your concern, you repellent brats. Go away!"

"But it has been our concern for ages, Father," Anne said, taking a seat as if settling in for a long stay and inspecting a dish of comfits on the table by her side.

"Indeed it has," Amelia agreed. "Why, we have been trying this age to get the two of you together."

"Can that be why you ran away to the gypsies, twins?" the duke asked, his voice stern.

Anne nodded, her mouth full of toffee; her twin was forced to say, "Yes, that is why we went. Juliet was not visiting Severn anymore, and we had no other way to promote the match."

The duke's sudden silence was ominous until the twins noticed that Juliet's eyes were bright with amusement.

"How happy we will all be!" Anne said, swallowing the toffee at last.

"A-l-l?" her father asked, his voice full of undertones.

"But of course, Father," Amelia explained. "Now that you and Juliet are going to be married, we will be together all the time."

"Good Lord," the duke said weakly, "I never thought of that."

Anne nodded. "We wouldn't want Juliet to be bored," she said simply.

The lady under discussion turned her head away and covered her mouth with a shaking hand as the duke said in his haughtiest voice, "Please do not concern yourselves. I can assure you that Juliet will never be bored when she is alone with me. You may leave the matter in my hands; I believe I am capable of seeing to it without your assistance. Besides, in a very few years, you will be thinking of your own marriages."

"Oh, we are in no hurry, are we, Melia?" Anne asked.

"Not at all. In fact, we may not marry for years and years and years," Amelia said with a sunny smile. "It will be so much more pleasant at Severn now, won't it, Anne?"

As her twin nodded, the duke asked, "More pleasant? Whatever do you mean?"

"Why, you are sure to be better-tempered now, just like Bob Randall, the groom. He was so cross before he married Lucy, but now he's all smiles. I expect Juliet will make you happier, too," Anne told him. "It will be such an improvement!"

The duke buried his face in his hands for a moment, and then he straightened up and slipped one arm around Juliet's waist to pull her close to his side.

"Go away!" he ordered, his drawl noticeably absent.

"Sir? Us?" both twins said together, looking surprised.

"Yes, who else? Go away! At once!" the duke commanded, sounding hard-pressed to keep his temper. "You have not only insulted me—good Lord, a groom! —I am reminded that the lady has not agreed to our marriage as yet, and if she hears any more of the delightful treats *you* have in store for her, she may never do so."

"Juliet is not so silly, why—"

"You will marry him, won't you, Juliet? He is not really so *very* disagreeable, and we—"

"*Go!*" the duke bellowed.

Amelia stole another glance at his stern, set face, and then she grabbed her twin's hand. Without a word, the two of them scurried to the door.

As one, they turned to make their curtsies, and then, in a voice stiff with offended feeling, the Lady Anne said, "We shall return at a more propitous time."

"Propitious," her elders corrected her in unison.

"May we wish you both happy, sir, m'lady?" the Lady Amelia asked formally, her blue eyes hurt.

The duke raised his free hand and pointed to the door. "*Out!*" he said. "This instant!"

His daughters tilted their chins and about-faced. "We certainly know when we are not wanted, don't we, Melia?" Anne asked as they marched out the door.

"Certainly," Amelia agreed. "We are not two ignorant little scullery maids, you know. We will come back later."

"You will come back here at your peril," the duke called after them. He barely waited until the door closed behind them before he said as he took Juliet back in his arms, "You will say yes, won't you, love? I will not let them make your life a misery. I will send them to school, you will never even have to see them, I promise!"

He sounded so worried that she might even now refuse to saddle herself with such an onerous burden that Juliet hid a smile.

"They are a little more than a bride would expect to face, your Grace," she told him solemnly. "And then, of course, there is Charlie, and your two other sons as well. But perhaps if you can restrain all your numerous offspring from accompanying us on our wedding journey, I might be tempted to say yes."

She smiled at him, and he caught up her hand and turned it so he could kiss the soft inner skin of her wrist. "Say yes, Juliet, say yes," he whispered.

The Cartel clock on the mantel ticked off several seconds, and he held his breath, his dark eyes intent now on her face, as she leaned back in his arms to study him.

Juliet saw his love for her blazing in his eyes, and she felt a warm tide deep within her that turned and twisted and spread until she felt quite weak. Yet still she hesitated. She knew very well, in spite of his humble pleading now, that in some ways William Fairhaven would always be the Dreadful Duke—a proud man, prone to sarcasm and a belief in his own omnipotence. He would never suffer the fools of the world gladly, and he was sure to anger her sometimes with his hauteur and arrogance. It would not be easy to be the wife of the Duke of Severn, but she realized that nothing that promised such wonderful fulfillment could ever be had without a struggle. And he did love her, as she loved him. There might be storms ahead, but there was also glorious happiness in the life they would share together.

"Yes," she said at last. "I will."

What else she might have added was forever lost, for the duke picked her up in his arms and held her close so he could bury his face in her hair, murmuring of his love. And then those warm, wonderful lips were on hers again, and the twins and all the other young Fairhavens and their multitudinous problems faded into oblivion.

At least for now.

About the Author

Although Barbara Hazard is a New England Yankee by birth, upbringing, and education, she is of English descent on both sides of her family and has many relatives in that country. The Regency period has always been a favorite, and when she began to write seven years ago, she gravitated to it naturally, feeling perfectly at home there. Barbara Hazard now lives in New York. She has been a musician and an artist, and although writing is her first love, she also enjoys classical music, reading, quilting, cross-country skiing, and paddle tennis.

SIGNET Regency Romances You'll Enjoy